We Move

——

We Move

Gurnaik Johal

———

First published in Great Britain in 2022 by
SERPENT'S TAIL
an imprint of Profile Books Ltd
29 Cloth Fair
London EC1A 7JQ
www.serpentstail.com

Lines from 'Object Permanence' from *Ordinary Beast* by Nicole Sealey © 2017 by Nicole Sealey.
Used by permission of HarperCollins Publishers.

1 3 5 7 9 10 8 6 4 2

Typeset in Tramuntana Text by MacGuru Ltd
Designed by Nicky Barneby @ Barneby Ltd

Printed and bound in Great Britain by Clays Ltd, Elcograf S.p.A.

A CIP catalogue record for this book is available from the British Library.

ISBN 978 1 78816 946 2
eISBN 978 1 78283 920 0

FSC
www.fsc.org
MIX
Paper from
responsible sources
FSC® C018072

For my parents and grandparents

Contents

——

Arrival

—

THE MAN WAS HERE ABOUT THE CAR. Chetan knew this day would come, but he'd allowed himself to hope. They both looked at the empty drive.

'My wife,' Chetan said, not sure when Aanshi would be back. 'We just needed a few things.'

It occurred to him to ask for proof that the man knew Divya. The man nodded and pulled a small picture out of his wallet. Chetan recognised the photo; he and Aanshi had seen it when stalking Divya on Facebook. It showed the couple on holiday, kissing in front of the pyramids. Chetan invited him in, and the man carefully put the photo back into his wallet.

Chetan took him into the kitchen, the front room a mess. The man asked questions about Divya that Chetan had imagined the police asking. When did she drop the car off? How long did she stay? Were there any signs that something was wrong?

But there'd been no investigation. She wasn't technically missing.

'We were at work when she arrived,' Chetan said, offering the man a seat. 'She posted the keys through the door. We'd agreed that I'd pick her up when she landed the next Sunday.'

Living this close to the airport, friends were always using their drive. Some relatives only seemed to visit for the parking space. 'Why don't you get a car?' they'd say, as if the idea had never crossed Chetan and Aanshi's minds. They got around fine as it was, riding the same bus in opposite directions for work. Cars only lost value. Plus, there was Aanshi's whole environment thing.

'Point being,' Chetan said to the man, 'it really wasn't a problem saying yes to another person, even if we'd never met.'

Divya was the sister of a good friend, and in Chetan's book, that meant something.

Chetan had driven Divya's car to the airport on the Sunday her return flight was due. He arrived at the short-stay pick up and texted her. He waited long enough that he was ushered on. He made a loop and pulled up a second time. He phoned her but didn't get through. He was told to move again and resigned himself to paying for parking.

Inside Arrivals, he found her flight on the boards. It had landed in good time.

There was nowhere to sit. He looked around, matching the people waiting with the people arriving. She still hadn't answered any of his texts. He phoned her sister, Anu.

'Says it landed fine.'

'I don't get it.'

'Maybe she missed the flight?'

'But why wouldn't she tell you?'

'Her phone could have died. She might have lost it.'

He waited until the next flight from Athens landed and left. The final figure on the parking you wouldn't believe. He drove home in a right mood. When he arrived, Aanshi was on the phone to Anu. Divya's fiancé had received a message: 'I'm just not ready.'

Days passed, the car out front.

'Was probably cold feet.'

'Or she's run off with someone.'

'What if she's escaping something? Committed a crime.'

'Maybe she's an undercover spy.'

'What if she's been, like, kidnapped?'

They called Anu again to ask her if there was any news of her sister.

The next Saturday, they did their food shop. Normally, they'd take the bus, but the car was just sitting there. Aanshi drove and Chetan put the radio on. God, how long since they'd listened to the radio? At the supermarket, he picked one of the big trolleys. They walked around with the same list they brought every week. But they were no longer limited to what they could carry.

'Let's go wild.'

'I love you like this.'

They were home in record time.

They didn't touch the car again all week. What would happen if Divya turned up out of the blue and it was gone? They spent the evenings cooking lavish meals and ate in front of an old sitcom they were watching for the first time. They froze the leftovers, wanting something new each night.

On the weekend, they decided to go to IKEA, a nightmare on the bus. While Chetan hummed along to the radio, Aanshi went through the glove box. She put on a pair of glasses that must have been Divya's.

'They suit you.'

'I always wanted glasses. I used to lie at the opticians.'

He'd heard this one before.

'I don't know how they knew I was faking. It never worked.'

They got a space right by the entrance. Usually, they split up to cover more ground and met at the checkout, where they'd veto each other's choices. But this time they stuck together. He didn't even need to persuade her on the plates. And when she found an office chair that was just perfect, he didn't look at the price. They loaded everything into the car and assembled it all that night.

Another week passed with no news of Divya. Aanshi settled on the story that she'd found someone. Chetan on the story that she was running from something.

He beat the dust off their picnic blanket and put it in the boot. She wanted to drive. He blew on the coffee until it was the temperature she liked, and then held the thermos out for her to take sips on quieter stretches. They sang along to whatever was playing on Magic.

They'd been meaning to visit Windsor for years. Someone took their photo in front of the castle. They wandered around a park and cleared a patch of grass for their picnic.

'Did you ever play conkers as a kid?' Aanshi said, putting a few in her bag. 'I'll show you when we get home. We used to have these huge tournaments at school.'

'You've never told me that before.'

'I wasn't any good. We started putting bets on the games and they got banned.'

She rested on his chest after lunch and they stayed like that, doing nothing. It was calming to feel the weight of her on him, this whole other human.

That week, he drove her to the care home in the mornings and picked her up when school finished. In the car, they discussed their students and patients. Chetan was almost grateful for the traffic.

They made plans to drive down to the coast. They were supposed to leave tomorrow. But here was the man about the car. The man who was supposed to marry Divya.

Chetan didn't know what to say. He listened to the TV playing in the front room. He made tea and arranged some biscuits on one of the new plates, which felt a ridiculous thing to do as soon as he put it down on the table.

'We filled up the tank,' he said.

He needed somewhere to look and turned to the window, setting his eyes on the two conkers from Windsor hardening in the sun. They hadn't got around to playing with them yet. He thought he saw the car pass outside and imagined Aanshi deciding to drive away. He imagined a sitcom in which he and the man formed an unlikely friendship – the two of them, bonded by abandonment, helping one another rebuild their lives.

Aanshi pulled up. She turned the engine off but stayed in the driver's seat, hands on the wheel. How rare to see her without her seeing him, to get a glimpse of the person she was beyond him.

'Here she is,' he said, finally.

It wasn't until the man stepped outside that Aanshi moved. She opened her door, confused about the stranger who had emerged from their house. The man explained, and she fidgeted with the keyring. She handed him the keys, apologising, and joined Chetan in the doorway. They watched the car go. He didn't ask her why she wasn't carrying anything, why there were no shopping bags. He didn't need to know.

She took some leftovers from the freezer to thaw. Chetan ate a biscuit, ruining his little pattern. There was laughter from the other room. He turned off the TV.

'What was he like?' she said.

'Nice enough. Not much of a talker.'

'Wonder what he did to make her leave.'

'If we're being honest, he was punching.'

'Coming from you.'

He drew her in, laughing. 'If you left me, where would you go?'

'Nowhere far. Maybe Mum's.'

'The whole world open to you and you go to your mother's?'

'I'd be sad. And you?'

'Somewhere with a beach. A desert island would be perfect. I think if I left you, I'd want to leave everything.'

She sat at the computer and put some music on. They paid for train tickets to Brighton – you wouldn't believe how much – and then sorted dinner. The kuzhambu they made last week came out in a slab in the pan. They stood together as it cooked, watching it become liquid again.

'Tomorrow,' she said, 'I want you to act like you've just met me.'

'Like I'm sixteen?'

'I want you to ask if the seat next to me is free and then work up the courage to talk to me. You'll say that you've never been to Brighton, and I'll agree to show you around. You'll buy lunch and I'll buy dinner.'

'Will I be myself?'
She looked at him, a whole other person.
'Yes.'

The Red River

—

If I were a penman and could write a fine hand
I'd write my love a letter from this foreign land
I'd send it by the water just for to let her know
That I think of Pretty Saro wherever I go.

'Pretty Saro' (Roud 417)

21 October 1972

'CHAK LA!' ONKAR SAID, slamming down his winning hand.

'Quiet, will you,' Balwant said, picking up his cards. 'If the landlady hears.'

It had been a decade since they had last played, back in Jalandhar when Onkar was a boy and Balwant, his oldest cousin, was leaving for England. Now here they were in London, reunited, and Onkar was three games up.

Balwant shuffled. He'd replaced two missing cards with carefully torn pieces of paper, seven of hearts, queen of clubs.

'I'm out of practice,' Balwant said. 'If this was Solitaire, different story.'

Onkar lit a cigarette on the tealight – their one small gesture to Diwali. He leant out of the window to smoke, taking in the view. Balwant had described the area in his letters, detailed the shops and the people and the clothes and the music and the food and the buildings. But the reality didn't match the vivid pictures his words had conjured; it wasn't that Balwant was lying or exaggerating, there was just so much space between all those things. All Onkar could see now was an empty street. He'd read in *The Times* that most of the universe and almost everything in it was made up of emptiness, that you could condense the human race to the size of a sugar cube. A light turned on in a room across the road. Letting out a long breath, he watched a man walk into the room, pick up something and walk out, leaving the light on.

He put his cigarette out – the seventh one he'd ever smoked. He wondered at what point he'd lose count. When he landed yesterday, several oceans between him and his mother, the first thing he did was buy a pack of cigarettes. He picked the brand at random and tucked the little box into his rolled-up t-shirt sleeve, like he'd seen in the movies.

Back at the table, he ran his hand over the wood. This was where Balwant had written all those letters. Most of the time they were to his wife, his mother, or his son, but there would often be little asides for Onkar. Like a few months ago, he'd asked if Onkar could take his son to the cinema for him to watch a film he'd seen recently in Southall. The boy had babbled away the whole walk home, talking about his dad as if he were some god, invisible, all-powerful. Onkar got engaged to Renu a few weeks later, and it was decided that he'd move to England before the wedding. He made a mental pact not to turn out like his old cousin; he'd be with Renu soon.

Balwant dealt one final round and they played in silence. Onkar won and Balwant went to sleep. Left at the table, Onkar tried to write his first letter to Renu. What to say? Maybe he should wait until he had real news, until he'd gone to the Labour Exchange and got a job. He started to write a sentence and looked up. He stared at the tealight, thinking back to the first time they met, at Renu's house, and how the power had cut out. He caught her eye in the dark while she went looking for candles, a slight smile neither of their parents would see. Once the candles were lit, their parents talked. He and Renu both picked the Parle-G over the barfi. She took the smallest bites. She fiddled with her kara, clockwise and anti-clockwise, and it reflected shapes onto the dark ceiling.

He rolled up his failed letter and lit the edge of the paper on the dying tealight. The paper burned for a few seconds before he blew it out. Then there was a shrieking sound. Balwant sprang out of bed.

'The bloody alarm! Out of my way, will you.'

He rushed over to a plastic box in the ceiling and waved his hands underneath it. Onkar could hear movement downstairs, the landlady. He opened and closed the window over and over, so that, to someone passing outside who might happen to look up, it looked like a small struggling wing.

4 March 1978

Fifteen minutes after she'd landed, it still felt like Renu was gaining height. Her stomach was agitated with excitement. Onkar was probably already here, somewhere in the airport. He'd written that he'd be wearing a red tie. She wondered what they'd talk about first – the flight? She tried to think of something intelligent to say about it. Onkar was an intelligent man – when her family had visited his, there were two different newspapers on the table. She imagined him reading the news in the mornings, saying intelligent things about politicians. On the plane, she'd read the paper three times, trying to memorise different stories in case they came up in conversation. She could talk about the Internal Settlement in Rhodesia. She could talk about the plans for the Panama Canal. The world seemed so big in the papers, but it felt a lot smaller now. Renu was here, on the other side of the planet, in the same amount of time it had taken her masi to travel from her pindh to Jalandhar to see her off. Masi had brought a little dog-eared book about marriage that she showed to Renu when her mother left the room. There were diagrams of what to do at night. Renu couldn't help but laugh.

'I'm serious,' Masi said. 'You do this one and you'll have a long, happy marriage.'

'Masi!'

'Especially with all this time. It's important.'

Her mother returned and Masi hid the book.

Renu wondered if she should hug Onkar when she saw him, or if they needed to wait until after the wedding.

The officer finally called her forward.

'I'm here to get married,' Renu said, when he asked about her plans.

'Look a little old to be getting married,' the officer said. 'When's the wedding?'

'Saturday.'

'I'm going to need you to wait here.'

He left his booth, and she checked her hair in her reflection. Looking down, she spotted a split end. Concentrating, she pulled on both strands until one broke off.

The officer returned with a man in a white coat. 'To ensure the validity of your story, we'll need to undergo some tests.'

Renu wasn't sure of validity or undergo. 'I'm sorry, I don't exactly understand.'

'Course not.' He sighed. 'Look, we get all sorts calling themselves fiancées. So, there's a procedure. Few medical tests. No time at all.'

'Medical tests?' she said. She looked at the man in the white coat. 'With him?'

15 August 1976

The bed was Onkar's from seven. Balwant and Sanjeev had it during the day, both working nights. He showered, ate his porridge and showered again. He covered himself in soap three times. Under the water, he thought of Renu. He imagined her in the shower. He couldn't fully remember her face; it had been so long. He waited for his erection to die down before heading to the bedroom.

The heat was unbearable. Sanjeev and Balwant were sleeping without the duvet, and they seemed oddly exposed on the bed – Sanjeev, so tall, curled up like a child, Balwant with both his hands on his stomach. Onkar boasted about getting the bed to himself, but sometimes seeing them together, he was almost jealous.

Balwant was losing his hair, always leaving grey strands on the pillow that Onkar would have to shake off. Sanjeev's hair had already grown out into an unkempt mess. When he'd arrived a few months ago, Balwant and Onkar had cut it for him, not wanting him to go through the embarrassment of the barber's. It was easier this way, they'd explained, having heard stories about the warehouse where he'd landed a job.

'Come on. Up.'

'Ugh,' Balwant said. 'You stink.' Sanjeev woke. 'Seriously, you smell disgusting.'

Balwant made caps for soap dispensers. Sanjeev loaded lorries. Onkar worked the gutting spot at a slaughterhouse. This morning, he'd squeezed the unformed shit out of the intestines of not one but two pigs.

'I've showered twice.'

'And you make the whole room smell.'

'It can't go on.'

'If either of you can get me a job, I'll happily quit.'

'I could try and get you some industrial-grade soap.'

'You could start wearing perfume.'

'You two will be late for work.'

They wouldn't get up. Onkar lay down between them and they jumped out.

He tried and failed to go to sleep. The moment from last week played and replayed in his mind. He'd sliced a cow open and a baby fell out. Onkar had a reputation with the foreman for not losing his nerve like the others and didn't want to squander it. He'd picked up the foetus – it was so light – and tossed it into the discard skip. It had eyes. He tried to think of something else, and focussed on the idea of Renu, which was increasingly abstract, a play of light on the ceiling. It had been a while since he'd written to her.

He woke to the smell of incense. That day, he had to cover for someone who'd quit, and spent hours slitting throats, blood spraying up the tiled walls and running in rivers across the floor, where it bloated the old drains. He timed himself while chopping, trying to calculate the amount of money he was earning per head by dividing his wage packet. He thought about the house prices he'd circled in the paper. How many bricks made a house? He took a guess, calculated the number of heads per brick. He kept going, head after head, brick after brick, comforted in the knowledge that, with each passing moment, he was a little closer to Renu.

4 March 1978

The man in the white coat smiled. There was a spot of dried blood on his chin. His breath was heavy. Renu always expected doctors to be healthy. They arrived in a small medical room.

'What do you call them, are they trousers?' he said. 'Can you take them off?'

'Excuse me?'

He did a lot of talking. Renu didn't know every word. It felt like they might not let her through, might send her back. She thought of Onkar. She thought of Saturday. She took off her clothes.

After putting on a pair of blue gloves, he squeezed something onto a bit of cotton and glanced at her. She turned all her energy into holding her body perfectly still. She thought of Rhodesia. She thought of Panama. She didn't blink. She didn't make a sound.

The doctor inserted two fingers into her vagina.

She watched a bead of sweat slowly run down his neck. Her fists were clenched so tight that, when it was finally over, and she opened them, she could see the indents her nails had left, all in a line on her palm, like waves. She had to take her bra off for an X-ray. She lay on a bed and the machine moved over her. It was another test for signs of previous pregnancy.

Finally, she could put her clothes back on. He left her in the room and got the results that would determine whether or not she was a virgin. She wondered if the machine could tell him that she'd kissed another man two years ago. It had been months without a letter from Onkar, and she'd thought he'd abandoned her. She imagined him with a British wife in a big house, laughing at the idea of her waiting miles away. It was the man who delivered her father's medication. She'd seen him every fortnight for years. Spending all day tending to her deteriorating father, the sight of the man, smiling at the door – she was only human. In that moment of weakness, she didn't think about Onkar, didn't even care that the man was from a different caste, there was only the space between them, closing in. She imagined the doctor ringing Onkar to tell him she was unfaithful. She'd be returned, arriving in that empty house a disgrace.

The doctor opened the door and took her back to the officer.

'She's good to go.'

'You've got three months. Understand?'

She walked off, joining the crowd heading down the hall. Seeing the exit, she stopped. People continued passing around her. She fixed her chunni, brushed off a fallen strand of hair from her shoulder. She picked up her suitcase and stood as straight as she could before walking into Arrivals. She held her head up and began to smile, because, with every step she took, she was a step closer to Onkar.

*

Onkar didn't know what to do with his hands. He should have left the flowers at home. He'd bought a vase at the market, and new sheets, and a little ceramic dolphin. She'd told him, in one of her letters, how she thought she'd spotted a river dolphin in the Sutlej at sunset, but when she got a little closer, she realised it was a bin bag.

In her most recent letter, she sent him a shopping list – she wanted to cook for him when she arrived. He'd gone to Fruits of Paradise and stocked up. It was the biggest shop he'd done in years. He'd dropped the food off at his house – *his house!* – and went down the Broadway with Balwant and Sanjeev to buy a suit. It was only when Onkar took his clothes off to get measured and saw himself in the dusty mirror that he realised how much weight he'd lost.

He tried to put his left hand in his pocket, but it was still sewn shut. He broke the seam open with his fingers, realising he should have cut his nails. It was clear that everyone from the Indian flight had already come out, there were only goreh walking through the gates. Where was she? She said in her letter that she'd be wearing a yellow chunni. She might have already passed through, neither of them recognising one another. Maybe she was waiting outside at the taxi rank thinking he'd stood her up. He thought about going to look but was scared that in the minute he was gone, she'd arrive. So he paced around the hall, glancing up at the pigeons in the rafters. He counted the number of people coming through the gate. They had likely come off the flight from Canada. He estimated the number of miles it was to Toronto, and then multiplied that by the number of passengers. He tried to estimate the square footage of the room. The number of builders who had worked on the site times the wage they likely earned times the time it took to build.

He spotted a glimpse of yellow in the crowd. Renu. He tightened his grip on the flowers. They walked towards each other. He stretched out his arms, overcome with joy, and held her tight. He buried his face into her shoulder; there was a slight chemical smell of what must have been shampoo. He tried to make sure he didn't cry. When her grip on him loosened, he finally let go, and they laughed. He gave her the flowers and picked up her suitcase. He wanted to hold her hand but didn't want to embarrass her. They walked to the bus stop, and he asked about the flight.

'I read this really interesting piece about the situation in Rhodesia.'

'Oh really,' he said, trying to remember where Rhodesia was. 'Crazy times we're living in.'

They got on the bus, and she continued talking in Punjabi. He could feel people staring.

'Look,' he said, gently. 'It's better that we're not so loud.'

'Oh.'

'It's not you. It's just here people like quiet.'

She looked out the window. He listened to people chatting behind them. After a few stops, he opened his palm for her to hold.

24 May 1980

'Heads for bride,' Renu said. 'Tails for groom.'

Renu flipped the coin as Onkar parked the car. 'Okay, we're on the girl's side.'

They came up with their characters. Today, Renu had three children and Onkar owned a car dealership. She was an heiress, distantly related to Maharaja Ranjit Singh, and he had studied at Oxford University. Today, they'd been married eight years.

It was the third wedding they'd gate-crashed together, but the thrill was yet to wear off. They walked right in.

The tables were covered with paper sheets, like hospital beds. The family was clearly cheap: off-brand mixers and a DJ instead of a band. They took the table by the toilets, hoping they'd be left alone. Renu looked around for any customers that might recognise them. Onkar poured her a drink when no one was looking, and she quickly filled the glass with cola. She rested her foot against his. Unfortunately, a family joined them, hell-bent on talking. Renu sipped away as they got Onkar going.

When the starters arrived, they were talking about Thatcher. Which meant a conversation about unemployment, which meant Onkar gesturing with a half-eaten spring roll.

'They don't have jobs because they don't want to work.'

'It's lazy people, this country.'

The man started talking about 'the Pakistanis and the Blacks'. Renu watched Onkar nod, finishing his spring roll and starting another. He never stopped eating. Renu took a sip, thinking about how, when there were Black people in their butcher shop, Onkar would appear and stand with her by the till. Normally, you couldn't get him out of the back. Renu would be the one to go back and forth, 'Sirloin, darling. Lamb chop, darling.'

'They come here and want everything on a plate.'

The happy couple finally arrived, and everyone stood and clapped. The music began and Renu adjusted her chair to watch the dance floor.

Onkar and the man went to the open bar. The man's wife started to talk.

'Do you have any of your own?' she asked, nodding at her kids, playing with their food.

'Three,' Renu lied. 'Two boys and a girl.'

'Are they here?'

'I left them with their nanny,' she said, using her telephone voice. 'It's nice for me and my husband to get a night out once in a while.'

The dholki arrived, cutting their conversation off, and the bhangra began. Only a few women went up to dance, and they were split from the men as if they were at the Gurdwara. Onkar reappeared, offering his hand.

'Dance, darling?'

She could feel people watching and she loved it. It didn't matter at all what they thought, no one here knew them. They were the only couple on the dance floor. She held Onkar's hand and he twirled her around. The disco ball was taped in place. Christmas tinsel, foil streamers. It was a scene straight from her daydreams, those long years of waiting, Onkar turning from reality to fiction in her head. And now here they were, together, and nothing felt real. Look at him, arms outstretched, grinning in multi-coloured light. See him move.

They were escorted out by the bride's brothers and found their car blocked in on all sides. They were in hysterics. Onkar managed to fit his arm through the half-open window to reach his cigarettes.

He carried her heels while they walked home. There was a specific thrill in being barefoot on the pavement. It felt like she was walking through Southall naked.

4 March 1978

Arriving at the house, their house, Onkar gave Renu the keys.

'I want you to do it.'

She unlocked the door for the first time.

'Our door,' he said. 'Our hallway, our kitchen.'

He watched her run her hands over different surfaces. There was a burn mark on one of her knuckles he hadn't noticed before, or hadn't heard about, or had forgotten. The ingredients she'd requested were out on the counter.

'You don't have to start straight away,' he said, as she looked through the drawers for a knife. 'Let's relax.'

'It's okay. You need a good meal,' she said. So she'd noticed. His skinniness probably repulsed her. 'I've wanted to do this a long time,' she said.

She started to cut the onions and he took the chicken out of the fridge. She gave him a look.

How had he forgotten her vegetarian parents? 'We don't have to,' he said.

'No, if you eat it, I'll eat it. You have it often?'

He hadn't eaten any meat for months, saving up for the house and the flight. When he'd realised how much he could save, he started to fast every other day, almost enjoying the feeling of hunger, of putting something bigger before him. It made him feel like he was in control. He'd quit smoking. Hadn't had a drop in over a year. He wasn't going to be like the others, lazy, going nowhere, ending the week with as much as they started with. They'd come to the slaughterhouse smelling of alcohol, of money down the drain. But today, he'd wanted something to mark the occasion. And in his new suit, he'd gone down to his friend's butcher shop and asked for their best bird.

She tentatively took her first bite.

'You won't burst into flames.'

They ate in silence and listened to the neighbours argue. The walls were thin. Onkar had got so used to being able to prepare exactly what he was going to say to her in their letters that it was hard to spark a spontaneous conversation. He kept editing himself in his head and ended up saying nothing.

She wouldn't let him near the washing up. He wanted to touch her, to wipe away the suds that had splashed up her forearm. She'd taken off her kara to do the dishes, and he picked it up, spinning it round and round.

She took the longest shower. Onkar sat by the bathroom door, listening to the sound of the water. He calculated how many hours were left until 11.30 on Saturday morning, when they were booked in at the Gurdwara. How many minutes, how many seconds. The water finally stopped and he got up. Downstairs, he paced the kitchen, listening to the sounds of her above. He washed his face with cold water, wiped down the counter. The place was spotless. Balwant and Sanjeev had come over last night and the three of them had cleaned and cleaned.

'So, how will it work?' Sanjeev had said, on his knees, polishing the floor. 'You know, will you wait?'

'Quiet,' Balwant said.

'Of course. It's only a few days. It's been years, I can do a few days.'

'Have you done it before?' Sanjeev said.

Onkar squeezed the water out of a cloth.

'You talk too much,' Balwant said. 'Pass the bleach, will you.'

Renu came down, fully dressed.

'Tea?' she said.

Her hair was an even deeper black wet. It darkened the colour of her chunni around her shoulders.

'Actually,' he said, after a pause. 'I'm tired.'

'Oh.'

'You must be, too. With time difference.'

She was very still. He took her hand and led her upstairs. He could feel her bones. He had a sudden thought that if he tried, he could break them just by squeezing.

She sat on the edge of the bed and didn't move. He opened the window and leant against the sill, the evening breeze cooling his back. She was looking down at her lap.

Weren't they, essentially, already married? For all intents and purposes, they'd been husband and wife for years.

She finally met his gaze. She looked cold.

He shut the window and sat next to her. He slowly put his arm around her, and she relaxed, resting her damp head on his shoulder. They lowered back onto the bed. He wished he'd taken off his suit jacket, but he didn't want to move – she seemed so calm. Her breathing steadied and he assumed she'd fallen asleep. He looked up at the light that was still on, that would still be on when he woke in the morning, in his new suit and his polished shoes.

23 October 1984

The day before Renu and Onkar opened their second butcher shop, they went to the Gurdwara. Karan sat with his dad but walked over to join Renu after a few minutes. He played with the end of her chunni. His joora was already askew. He was almost four.

'Shush,' she said, fixing his hair. 'Go and sit with your dad.'

'Why's the man shouting?' he whispered, looking up at the front.

There was a series of speeches about the worsening situation in Delhi. They were talking about Operation Blue Star. They were talking about Khalistan. Normally on Diwali, there was just kirtan. But since the summer, everything was politics.

'Sit with your dad.'

Renu had been hoping that they could just do a quick matha tekna and get out. There was so much work still to do for the opening. But the speeches continued, and she could see Onkar across the hall, hands crossed on his large stomach, getting riled up with the rest of them. When she started to listen herself, she felt a burning anger. She wished there was some way to act, something she could do.

The speech ended and the speaker took a deep breath before roaring out a jaikara: 'Jo bole so nihal!' *Whoever utters shall be fulfilled.* The entire congregation shouted back. 'Sat sri akal!' *God is truth.* 'Jo bole so nihal!'
Renu screamed back with everyone else. 'Sat sri akal!'
'Jo bole so nihal!'
She thought of the images they'd seen on the news. 'Sat sri akal!'
'Jo bole so nihal!'
Turning off the TV when Karan was in the room. 'Sat sri akal!'
Someone in the crowd did the next jaikara. 'Jo bole so nihal!'
The letter her mother sent. 'Sat sri akal!'
Someone else took the lead. 'Jo bole so nihal!'
It was freeing to make so much noise. 'Sat sri akal!'
Renu had never thought of doing a jaikara before, but something came over her that day. She raised her fist in the air and shouted, the loudest her voice had risen since she'd arrived in London all those years ago. 'Jo bole so nihal!' she screamed.
The entire Gurdwara answered her. 'Sat sri akal!'

Onkar's friends came over for dinner and brought their kids. Renu, in the kitchen with the other women, watched the children play in the garden, an extra sugar cube in her tea. The men disappeared for a while and returned with fireworks. Celebrating didn't feel right to Renu, with everything going on, but Karan was so excited. They all headed out to the garden. The men lit rocket after rocket, each explosion a shock. Renu could hear the kids in the neighbouring gardens shouting. They were one of the earliest households in the area to get started, but after a few minutes, you could hear and see other fireworks going off across Southall. Smoke filled the night air, and the sound of fire multiplied. Bright reds and yellows. Karan wanted to light one, and Renu took him to the end of the garden and placed the rocket in the pile they'd made with surplus bricks. Holding his blue gloves, she helped him light the match. She held it to the fuse, and it took, starting to fizz. She picked him up and ran back towards the house. They heard the hiss and then the high-pitched squeal, looking up to see the most glorious display of light. Karan screamed; his voice drowned out by the explosion. How happy she was that he could be so loud, that he would never know quietness like she had.

Leave to Remain

——

GUJAN HAD A FREE.

'All right,' he said, walking into XFC.

'Say nothing,' Umer said, lifting the counter to let him through to the back of the chicken shop. Khalid was vaping on Baba Ji's stairs, fresh fade under his hairnet, 'Know Yourself' playing on a Beats Pill.

'All right.'

'Safe.'

Gujan headed up and let himself in. Baba Ji wasn't in his spot. The TV was off. The infusers and air fresheners that Mum put up weren't doing jack against the smell of fried chicken from downstairs.

He could barely remember a time before XFC. But his parents would often talk about Baba Ji's shop, how Gujan would sit on his Baba's lap behind the till. When he started walking, he'd follow him around, pretending to stock the shelves, a plastic banana here, an Action Man there. But these were their memories, not his. Gujan could only remember the shop through the things that survived it, his deck of Yu-Gi-Oh cards, a few shiny Match Ataxx, his limited-edition Ronaldo.

Gujan sat down on the sofa next to Baba Ji's armchair. 'Baba Ji, meh aagiya!'

He took out the paperwork. Mum had filled out the forms at their hotel in Spain and emailed them over. It was Gujan's job to print them at school, take Baba Ji to get his photo done and then mail it all off. He glanced over the forms, full of phrases that meant nothing. Settled Status. Home Office. Right of Abode. It was strange to see his Baba's full name, Sanjeev Singh Purewal, to see the facts of his life written out in block capitals. Date of birth, country of origin. He was a person like anyone else, but to Gujan, he was Baba Ji, part of the fabric of his own life, part of the furniture. He was always there in his spot.

Baba Ji came out of the bedroom wearing a suit. Gujan recognised it from the times he'd sat in his Baba's wardrobe, playing
hide-and-seek with his cousins. It had pinstripes, wide lapels. He
looked sharp. Gujan couldn't remember ever seeing him in anything other than kurta pyjama.

'Sat sri akal ji,' Gujan said, getting up to go.

Baba Ji held a tie in his hands. It'd been a while since he'd done
one, he said. Gujan lifted his collar. He was tall, but still only came
up to his Baba's chin.

'Thanks son,' Baba Ji said in English. He took a deep breath when
Gujan opened the front door, and held onto his arm as they went
down the stairs.

'Safe,' Khalid said.

When the 607 arrived, Baba Ji took out some change.

'They won't take that,' Gujan said in Punjabi. Baba Ji looked
confused. Gujan helped him onto the bus. 'Can I tap us twice?' he
asked the driver.

Baba Ji looked out the window the whole way to Sainsbury's.
Gujan hadn't clocked how long it had been since his Baba last left
the house until he heard how his parents were stressing about the
trip. It's fifteen minutes, Gujan had thought, he'll be fine.

'You're old enough now,' Mum had said on the phone from
Vigo, 'to know that your Baba isn't really all okay. It's a big deal he's
agreed to go.'

Did he have a choice? His parents would be out in Spain for
another few weeks. 'What happens if we don't send the forms?'

Their stop came up and they made their way into the supermarket. Baba Ji looked even paler in the bright light. The vitiligo
covered most of his face now, and there were only a few patches
of brown remaining on his hands. Gujan couldn't remember ever
talking about it.

Gujan helped him into the photobooth. He pressed shoot
and shut the curtain. Baba Ji looked like a different person to the

brown, clean-shaven man in his previous passport photo. Gujan could remember when, with no explanation, he started to wear a pagh and stopped shaving.

'It could be good news,' Dad had said. 'He might start going to the Gurdwara. Socialise.'

'It's just what old men do,' Mum had said. 'They turn at the end.'

When Dad left the room, she'd continued. 'You can't forget that your Baba loved his sharaab back in the day.'

That had always confused Gujan, the stories of him driving home drunk from weddings, of fights at last orders. It wasn't the man Gujan knew. One of his only memories of the shop was when the brick was thrown in and Baba Ji rushed him upstairs. The man Gujan knew calmly brushed up the shards of scattered glass and taped a flattened cardboard box over the hole in the window.

They got the bus back to the Broadway and, getting off at their stop, Baba Ji asked if they might go for a walk. Gujan texted Raveena to say he wouldn't make final period Maths. Baba Ji was walking faster now. Every time Gujan came to the Broadway, it looked different. He couldn't imagine how much had changed since Baba had last seen it. Baba Ji stopped at a little stall to buy steamed sweetcorn. They sat on a bench and shared the pot. Then, out of nowhere, he hailed a passing taxi and told Gujan to get in.

Gujan had never been in an actual black cab. He felt like a tourist. Baba Ji talked to the driver – he wanted to go to the trading estate. A few minutes later, they pulled up and the driver asked for fourteen pounds. Baba Ji took out his coins and Gujan tapped his card on the reader.

Almost every lot had its shutters down. Gujan remembered learning to ride his bike here, Dad taking him around the empty car parks, the quiet roads. Baba Ji led him round the back of a warehouse. Other than a few broken pallets, the place was empty.

'Fifteen years I worked here,' he said.

'And then the shop?'

'Then the shop.'

Baba Ji looked around, and when he seemed satisfied, they walked out of the estate. On the main road, Gujan turned towards the bus stop. But Baba Ji paused at a bank of Boris bikes.

'They're bikes that you can rent,' Gujan explained.

'Free?'

'No.'

'Cheap?'

Gujan had never cycled on a main road before. His seat was at an uncomfortable height, cars came way too close and revved at the lights, where he took too long to push off. He could imagine his parents getting mad, not just that he was cycling on busy roads, but that he'd allowed his Baba to. But the man looked so happy, breezing through the streets of Southall, pulling out ahead. They dismounted when they got to the bridge by the station, and they walked their bikes to the top.

'I used to have to cycle all the time. I always dreamed of getting a car. And then I got a car and I missed riding my bike.'

Gujan imagined Baba Ji at his own age now, cycling around. Then he imagined himself at his Baba's age. They got back on their bikes and freewheeled down to the bottom of the bridge. They stopped outside a pub.

'I used to come here Fridays.'

'And then the shop?'

'Then the shop.'

Baba Ji ordered two Doom Bars. Was he getting Gujan a drink? Did he know he was only 17? They didn't have that drink on tap. The bartender suggested something called Elvis Juice. Again, Gujan paid. They sat on two barrels against an exposed brick wall and drank.

XFC was empty when they got back. Umer had turned the TV up, candidates giving their finishing statements.

'All right,' Gujan said, ordering dinner.

'Say less, boss.' Umer looked at Baba Ji. 'Today's on the house.'

Back upstairs, Baba Ji sank into his spot and took off his tie. Gujan put on the news, pundits deciding who had won the debate. They ate together, wing by wing, until the bucket was nothing but bones.

Chatpata: Kaam

—

'First, we eat, then we talk.'

Guru Amar Das Ji to Emperor Akbar

TWO WEEKS AFTER HIS WIFE'S HEART ATTACK, Jagmeet made a mistake that would haunt him every month for several years. He decided to dye the patch of white hair under his chin. It's not like it bothered him, he didn't particularly care, but in this day and age, he thought, why not? He found one of Amrit's brushes in a clutch bag she'd taken to the last wedding they'd gone to. Lipstick, tissues, safety pins. What were you supposed to do with things like that, too small to keep? The bin felt so unceremonious.

He used the self-checkout at the supermarket for the first time ever that day, not wanting the cashier to see him with a box of Just for Men. The problem, he soon realised, was the dye was black in a way that the rest of his daree wasn't. When he applied it to the patch, he ended up with a dark streak under his chin. Commit to the mistake and it won't look like a mistake, his father used to say. When you play tabla, you mess up and people notice. But if you mess up and repeat the mistake, they think it's on purpose. Make the flaw a feature. He ran the brush through the rest of his daree.

He was reapplying the dye now, three years later. How long do you need to repeat a mistake for it to no longer feel like one? He was trapped: under the dye, the whole beard had turned white. If he stopped now, everyone would know he'd been colouring it all along; no one went this white overnight. Amrit would never have let him mess up like this. His daughters, Aman and Simran, were too polite. Aman, his eldest, had been living with him since her mother died, and must have seen the Just for Men in the bathroom countless times. But not a word.

He called Aman now to help do his pooni. She was getting her first

37

greys. How would that look, his daughter with white hair, and him with a jet-black beard?

She took her end of the pagh, and they each took a few steps back. They pulled the fabric taut, the length of the hall. Doing his pooni with his daughter, that was a simple joy. Before she left for culinary school all those years ago, the pooni was their weekly tug of war. She started doing it with him when she was a toddler. Simran, his youngest, joined in later, trying to copy her older sister. He could see it all so clearly, the two of them sliding across the laminate floor as he pulled, those slipper socks they used to wear.

Beard dry, pagh on, Jagmeet went downstairs. The herbs died not long after his wife, but he'd managed to keep the yoghurt alive. He put it in the fridge to set. He made tea for Aman and, listening out for the shower, opened the notebook she'd left on the counter.

When I think of the weekend, I think of parathe. I think of Mum rolling up atta into balls, little full stops to a long week. She didn't like anyone in her kitchen when she cooked. If we tried to help, we'd only stress her out. She was very particular about how they should be made, would rather throw an imperfect paratha out to the birds than feed it to anyone under her roof. She hated 'what they call parathe' at my dad's restaurant for instance. And when we'd drive back from visiting some relative's house, she'd always offer a critique of their cooking: 'What's the point of spending so long on saag if you won't add any flavour?' She was always more comfortable cooking for someone than she was eating their food.

Here, something was written and crossed out multiple times. Jagmeet could hear the shower turn off, but he carried on reading.

To me, the taste of a good aloo paratha is the taste of having nothing to do on a Saturday afternoon. It's the taste of watching cartoons with my little sister, Dad asleep on the sofa, kirtan playing on Mum's radio. Glazed in ghee, puffed up and flaky, that bread would literally dissolve on your tongue. Filled with a range of root vegetables, depending on Mum's mood, those parathe were the taste of the earth, they grounded you, and were so heavy with fat that you'd spend the next few hours in a kind of daze.

Jagmeet *worked* on Saturdays. He didn't know where she'd got the image of him sleeping on the sofa. Just like Aman, that. You never knew what she was going to put in print. Take an argument they'd had long ago – less an argument than a discussion. Aman had 'deconstructed' a pakora for a new menu and wanted him to taste-test. She knew better than to ask her mum. On the plate, little shards of fried potatoes, cauliflower and onions floated on some charcoal-black foam. Chutney was drizzled on top, red as ketchup.

'Where's the pakora?' he said.

'Just try it.'

It had the taste and texture of a good pakora. The sauce, he realised, really was just ketchup. What threw him off was the foam, it tasted just like Coke, and bubbled in his mouth long after he swallowed.

'Remember,' she said. 'When we had pakore, it was the one time we were allowed fizzy drinks.'

'I don't get it.'

'It's – I'm trying to recreate those memories in the dish.'

'Why not make pakore like your mum did and serve Coke with it? Then they'll taste just like you remember.'

'I can't recreate our home in the restaurant,' she said. 'So, I have to try and manipulate the dish so that it sparks similar feelings in the customer that it did in me then. Otherwise, it's just a pakora in an Indian restaurant, end of story.'

'I reckon customers would be happy if you just served really good pakore,' he said. 'And maybe more than one per plate!'

'Thanks, Dad.'

'It's like my Mata Ji always said. You know why gold is valuable? Because it doesn't change.'

And that was the line that appeared in an interview Aman had done for a food magazine: QUEERING PANEER: PUNJABI FOOD AS YOU'VE NEVER SEEN IT AT BROOKLYN'S AMBROSIA. He felt such pride seeing articles about her restaurant, seeing her name dotted throughout the text. In the interview, she said that she was still coming to terms with people saying her food was 'too much'. She said that 'less is more' was coded. She said that too-muchness pervaded every aspect of her 'Indian identity', everything from her food to her clothes to her accent, which had embarrassed her like nothing else as a child. The way her parents spoke, the thick lilt in the voice, how the tongue wrapped its way around the whole syllable. She talked about how the food of celebrated Indian chefs was still treated as kitsch. When critics praised it, they did so in a way that showed they could appreciate both high and low art. She was thinking about what it meant to make 'comfort food'. She wanted to overcome what she called the 'mango-fetish' westerners had when it came to Indian culture – you only had to wait so long, she said, when reading a western story about India, to come across a mango, a railway or a spiritual reawakening. She talked about chatpata, a mixture of spiciness, sourness and sweetness, and the balance central to cooking in a lot of Indian cuisines. Her aim, she said, was to hold both the future and the past on the plate.

'I don't get it,' Amrit had said, when he read the piece to her. 'They're saying the food is gay?'

'No, that's just the title.'

'Queer is gay, Jagmeet.'

'I think it's more about politics, maybe.'

'How can food be about politics? It's food.'

As he often did when his wife disagreed with him, he turned to the men in the chatroom for support. They were all impressed with the article, as they were whenever they heard about Aman. He'd been hesitant the first time he shared one of her podcast episodes with them – what if they outed him in the comments? Before that, they had no links to his real life, he was a username and an avatar.

When he first met the men in real life, they went out for a meal. Someone suggested meeting at the restaurant where Jagmeet worked, but he said they should go somewhere nicer, somewhere further away. It was a motley crew, ranging from men, like him, in their fifties to a few in their thirties and one in his twenties. They were all Sikh, and they were all gay. They got on around the table just like they did online. There was nothing, Jagmeet had thought, that compared to eating good food with good friends. How lucky he was to know so much joy.

The group met again, several months after Amrit passed, at the wedding of one of the member's sons. It felt wrong to be going to any kind of celebration in the same year as his wife's death, but they convinced him it would be good for him. He hadn't drunk like that in years. Amrit used to count his glasses, and without her around, he got carried away. The DJ pitted him and his friends in a dance-off with a group of auntiya. He lost all self-consciousness about his age that night, until they left and Karan, a man in his thirties, invited him home.

'I'm an old man,' Jagmeet said. 'You deserve so much better.'

'Just a drink–'

'Look, I can't.' His voice turned sharper than he would have liked. Karan left, embarrassed, or angry, Jagmeet wasn't sure. Karan didn't return his messages over the next few weeks, and when Jagmeet invited the group to Simran's wedding, Karan didn't turn up. He became less active in the chatroom, and then, out of nowhere, told them all that they needed to find their way back to Waheguru. He left the chat but Jagmeet found his same username and avatar in a comment on a forum that he followed.

RE: Gay thought. Sangat JI, need to help a brother of mine who has migrated to Europe. He got into the company of some Gay people and now he thinks he is gay. He seems to have been totally brain-washed and to ensure that no one points out a finger at a Keshdhari Sikh he has cut his hair. On his business trip to another country, he met another Sikh at a white collor level, who also turned out to be a gay. this thought has been cemented in him. I am helpless here as i feel it is against nature. With all the parades by the gay community and strong presence in Europe its very difficult for me to help him. Your thoughts and suggestions will be very helpful to many reading these posts.

We are all Waheguru's children, and we are all equal in His eyes. If he is a good Sikh, then he is a good Sikh, whether he is strait or gay. If he is a bad Sikh, he is a bad Sikh.

Address this issue as well in a non-threatening manner. Remind him of the sacrifices the great men and women have made over the centuries for all of us to live in freedom as Sikhs. Then, let it go.

I am not an expert but have gained some knowl;edge on this matter. I can only recommend true prayer to Waheguru to get him out of this problem. Ardas would be best solution.

WJKK WJKF, I would add that a lot of young people are needlessly experimenting to find out if they are gay. You're either gay or you are not. All this experimentation leads to confusion in life.

Gays are a tightly knit community. Young people who do not have strong attachments with family find support with them and start identifying with them. This is also gives them a feeling of being a victim and hence justifying their percieved discrimination against them. These are just my personal opinions.

I'm gay and proud, and a proud Sikh. There is very little enlighten-ment in this thread. I challenge anyone here to give me reference in the Granth where it forbids marriage between two men or two women. In an Indian culture that created the Kama Sutra, straight gay and lesbian kama sutra, surely the Gurus knew OF transcendent sexuality but it isn't mentioned specifically in any of the sacred texts. I didn't consciously choose to be gay, to disappoint my family or embarass them, and growing up I had no friends that were gay. From my sikh upbringing I didn't see sexuality as an issue. I wasn't having impure thoughts. Just natural experiences like every other child growing up. Let us not ignore the thousands of stories of asian men that marry women, only to have illicit affairs with other men "behind closed doors". What of the women? The children?

They are not said to be husband and wife, who merely sit together. They alone are called husband and wife, who have one light in two bodies.

I can only explain homosexuality as either lust taking over one's senses or perhaps God's way of population control. Either way, I don't think it has a place in Sikhism or our Gurudwaras.

If one is Gay they should keep it to themselves. I don't want my children seeing it and being de-sensitized to it. I want them to look at two men kissing and say 'groosss'. I don't want my children thinking it's another path they have the option to follow. If one of my children is gay, I want them to fight it like a disease, not be weak and accept it. What would the great Martyrs like Baba Deep Singh think of this topic? Or the hundreds of thousands of Sikhs who laid their lives in World War 2 think of a Gay Turban? Let's have a little respect here, gay people. Respect us. The Sikhs. The Brotherhood and Sisterhood of the pure. Image is everything. Do not tarnish it, just so you can make us more modern and urban. Stop it, right here.

The only epidemiological study to date on the life span of gay men concluded that gay and bisexual men lose up to 20 years of life expectancy.

Moderator Note: Kindly include some references to support your statements above.

For a moment of sexual pleasure, you shall suffer in pain for millions of days.

As Sikhs we should be tolerant of them, not alienate them or try to hurt them. Fair enough, if someone want to be gay behind closed doors, or maybe even have a cuddle in the street, tolerate them, let them be gay, I'm fine with it. But when someone tries to conflate the teachings of the Gurus with hippy liberalism, try and hold gay Anand Karajs, or tell me I'm ignorant and intolerant for fighting my case and giving my opinion, then I won't be too happy about it.

Gay or straight or bi or even asexual, it matters not, we are all creatures of Waheguru.

I think it is against nature and anything that is anti-nature is antisikkhism but it is just what i think.

I am sorry to say i don't agree with homosexuality. As on eof my brothers have pointed out in a previous post Guru Ji gives homosexuality no reference in any texts. That to me says it all.

Many peoples responses seem to come from personal opinions rather than objective logic. I don't think Gurbani cares if you are homosexual or heterosexual. If you are driven by sexual desires 'kaam' then either way your screwed. Sexuality should never be a major concern for a sikh. Because all types of sexuality homo or hetero leads you away from god. My argument is based on logic not personal opinions. FYI: I'm heterosexual.

Think of yourself as a tree!! A tree is a simple humble living thing (as Guru Ji would say) and it does not give itself too much importance thus once a year it gets flowers (akin to egg released and waiting

44

to be fertilized) and waits for pollination so that its flowers can become fruit. Just like that we are a humble living thing who need to use to reproduce and nothing else‼ Waheguru has given us kaam for reproduction and nothing else (realize this and you will have eternal happiness).

Jagmeet put the notebook back where he'd found it and busied himself with the tea. When Aman left home at 18, his wife moved into her empty bedroom. Simran, still at school, never mentioned the new sleeping arrangement. Jagmeet had welcomed the decision, sleeping in separate rooms was a weight off both of their shoulders. They'd shared a bed since their wedding night, years ago, a night that he still tried to forget.

Jagmeet drank heavily at their wedding reception, knowing what he'd have to face when the party was over. Amrit was quiet and young, weighed down with gold. He would have liked to do nothing to her and was sure that she would too. They could just talk. But he knew that her friends in the pindh would ask her about him, the quiet man, the survivor from the city, and they would ask about their first night together. He knew that those women would go on to tell their husbands, and soon everyone in the pindh would know he wasn't man enough to take his wife, not even on their wedding night. He drank and drank.

He turned the lights off. She didn't say anything the whole time. She lay on her back, but he told her to get on her knees and face away. He stood behind her, touching himself, trying to get hard. He thought of Hiten, of their last night together. Amrit tensed. He held her hips, imagining his hips being held, Hiten pushing him down onto the bed.

His memories of that time felt like they belonged to a different person. He and Amrit had sex a handful of times, and his fantasies of Hiten grew increasingly detailed. Finally, she said that she was pregnant. As soon as she started to show, he threw himself into religion. He avoided any of her advances under the pretence of expelling kaam from his life. But going to the Gurdwara every day, he prayed to feel more attracted to her. He wanted to love her. He wanted to stop thinking of Hiten.

He was so happy when Amrit gave birth to Aman. But his wife didn't like to hold the child. She barely slept at night and then would try to stay in bed all day. He cooked all their meals, and she ate more than he'd ever seen her eat. He felt like he would never understand her.

Aman started to talk and to walk. Sometimes he took her out in the fields while he worked, like his Mata Ji used to with him. Amrit started to connect with the child, to show signs of her normal self. Then she started to turn to Jagmeet at night. He stopped himself from flinching, and would say that he was tired, or that he wasn't feeling well. He knew she wanted a son more than anything.

One day, Amrit came home with two watermelons, and told Jagmeet to eat them both. Her friend, Mandeep, said that it would cure his impotence. She said it so earnestly that he ate both the melons and took her to bed. Hiten came right back into his thoughts. After several attempts, Simran was conceived.

Simran was born a British citizen in a hospital in London. They'd had a series of failed harvests on the farm, and an old friend had told Jagmeet that he was looking for a cook at his new restaurant in Southall. Jagmeet wanted to get as far away from Hiten, from his past, as he could. He was surprised at how willing Amrit was to move.

Jagmeet wanted London to be a fresh start. In focussing on the girls, on their futures, he could find a way of forgetting. He worked long hours at his friend's restaurant, cooking the house's one base sauce over and over, which they used in almost every dish. His daily rhythm was broken up by the occasional Friday night mistake – drinks at closing, a trip to central, a different man – repeated often enough that it was normal for him to be found on the sofa on a Saturday morning, not wanting to disturb Amrit when he came in. He hardly saw his family, and when he did get a chance to spend time with them, they would all seem to have changed into different people.

This was true, most of all, for Simran, his youngest. When Aman moved out to go to culinary school, a switch flicked in Simran. She started to ask about their lives in Punjab and began joining them on their trips to the Gurdwara. She skived off school to go to a march about the 1984 genocide when the new reports leaked and started to lecture Jagmeet and Amrit about the massacre. Amrit wasn't impressed, Simran should have been studying for exams. But Simran shunned going to university and said that she'd be taking a gap year to visit Punjab. Next thing Jagmeet knew, he was dropping her off at Heathrow for a flight to Amritsar.

When he picked her up a few months later, he didn't recognise her. She was wearing a pagh, kurta pyjama and a kirpan.

'Simran?'

'I know,' she said. 'Can you open the boot?'

He couldn't understand her transformation. He had to keep reminding himself it was a good thing. But his daughter, an Amritdhari?

'It's a cry for help,' Amrit said, coming into his bedroom that night to talk.

'You can't say that. That's not fair,' he said. 'She's found faith.'

'I think we should be worried.'

'We wanted the kids to be religious.'

The next morning was Vaisakhi. Jagmeet and Amrit were cooking, or rather, Jagmeet was helping with prep and doing his best to stay out of his wife's way. Simran came down to the kitchen with her hair out.

'Can you help me?' she said.

He tied her hair and they did the pooni together. The fabric was too large for her, so they trimmed it down. In front of the bathroom mirror, he tied it slowly, explaining each step. He looked at his reflection, and just like that, his little brother came back to him, the first night of the killings, in 84. That night, his mother had told

47

Jagmeet to undo his brother's pagh and to take off his patkah. His little brother cried while Jagmeet plaited his hair. He'd be safer if he looked like a girl, if he didn't look Sikh. A mob passed outside. They put his brother in girl's clothes that the neighbours had given them. He punched Jagmeet as he saw himself, suddenly transformed. Jagmeet's mother, brother and father left on the motorbike–

'Thanks, Dad,' Simran said.

He tried to stop remembering that night as he finished helping Amrit with the cooking and loaded the food into their car. They drove to the nagar kirtan in Southall and served chole bhature to passers-by out of the back of their car. No matter how much she stressed about cooking for Vaisakhi, he never saw his wife happier than when she was handing out all that food. Simran went off to join the procession and seeing a group of kids playing in the crowd, Jagmeet thought of Hiten, as he always did on Vaisakhi, remembering the two of them as children running through the city's nagar kirtan, trying to get as much food as possible.

'Happy Vaisakhi,' Aman said, coming into the kitchen. 'Should we eat before we start?'

'I've already started,' he said, nodding at the tadka in the pan.

'Should we eat before I start?' she said, taking out the parathe she'd made yesterday. She heated them up and served them with dahi and achar. It was mango achar, sweet, spicy and sour all at once. Too spicy. He didn't understand what it was that Aman had against mangoes. The thought of the fruit could still take him back to being a boy, to afternoons with Hiten. Every memory flowed back down to him in some way. They lived close to each other, and often took detours on the way to school to get breakfast from the chaat-wallahs. After school, they'd go on expeditions. Hiten wanted to be an explorer, and they'd head down to the railway tracks or to the river, beads of water clinging to the swirls of hair on Hiten's upper back, their clothes tied to a tree on the bank. Sometimes Jagmeet would sleep over at his house, and they'd talk deep into the night, making elaborate escape plans, head-to-toe in his bed, fighting for space. Jagmeet couldn't remember when they discovered the Castle, but they went almost every day after they found it. The Castle was an outcrop of old bricks, an abandoned building project by the tracks. It was surrounded by overgrowth, and they were never seen. They planted a kite as a flag and claimed the land as theirs. Jagmeet thought, now, of the day with the mangoes. Hiten brought them to the Castle after school. They rolled them in their palms, weakening the insides, getting the juice to flow. When the flesh had enough give, they bit off the tops, careful not to let a drop go to waste. They slowly squeezed the fruit, the golden juice sweet as nectar. When there was no juice left, they took out the pits and sucked on the hard stones. They threw the finished pits to the tracks and inverted the skins, eating the last hairy streaks of pulp. They both laughed, juice all over their faces. Then Hiten leant towards him, tongue out, and licked Jagmeet's face from his chin to his nose. They laughed. Jagmeet could feel Hiten's warm saliva drying on his skin. He turned and did the same to Hiten. They kissed.

After eating, Jagmeet made the filling. Aman made the puris, which puffed up into crispy spheres in the oil. She filled old Coke bottles with homemade imli water.

Every Vaisakhi since they'd arrived in England, Jagmeet and Amrit had taken food to the nagar kirtan. When her mother died, Aman had suggested they keep the tradition going. They loaded the car and set off. They parked as close as they could to the Broadway. It didn't take long for a queue to form around their car. Jagmeet sang along to the shabad as the procession headed slowly away. He cracked the puris and added the filling. Aman poured in the imli water and handed them out.

Watching the procession, Jagmeet spotted the signs. A group of young Sikhs were holding placards with the message *Never Forget 84*. They stood out amidst the celebrations, marching in silence.

49

Some of them were holding posters of Bhindranwale, others black-and-white photos of Sikhs being tortured in the street. He saw his younger daughter, Simran, holding up a picture of a body on fire.

He remembered his parents arguing about Bhindranwale in the early 80s. He was old enough to understand what they were talking about, but he didn't pay their conversations much mind. He knew the rough outline of what was going on: Bhindranwale and his Sikh followers wanted a more autonomous Punjab, some wanted a separate state altogether. Hiten called them terrorists.

Soon the news was in their streets. A bus was pulled over, an innocent man killed. Hiten was so angry he didn't come to the Castle for days. He said he was going out with other friends.

Then, in June 1984, the government carried out Operation Blue Star. They laid siege on Amritsar's Golden Temple, where Bhindranwale and some of his followers were based. The firefight lasted for hours; hundreds were murdered.

In October, Indira Gandhi, who'd ordered the attack, was assassinated by two of her Sikh bodyguards.

Jagmeet's father took his mother and brother on the motorbike. His plan was to drop them off at Mata Ji's farm and return for Jagmeet. They couldn't all fit on the small bike. All Jagmeet had to do was stay inside the house. He hid under his parents' bed. It wasn't long until he heard men outside. There was a hissing sound. He held his breath. The smell of smoke made its way into the house. As did the sound of shooting. Then there was a banging at the door. He prepared himself for what was about to happen. But no one kicked the door down, they just kept knocking.

'It's me. Hiten. Are you there?'

Jagmeet let him in. Hiten was out of breath, his eyes bloodshot. There was an S painted on the door.

'Come. Now. They're on their way through here.'

They headed to the Castle. He would not remember what he saw on the way.

Hiten didn't talk. When they arrived, Jagmeet tried to hold him, wanted to be held, but Hiten withdrew. His eyes were so red. He put his hand on Jagmeet's neck and ran it up his jaw and his cheek, up to his pagh. He pulled at the fabric until it came loose and dropped it to the ground. He undid Jagmeet's patkah and untied his hair, running his fingers through it, stroking it behind his ears. Jagmeet tried to kiss him.

There was no rhythm to the gunshots. The smell of burning came as the wind picked up. His pagh drifted across the ground in a gust. Hiten had a knife. He pulled Jagmeet's hair into one fist and tried to cut it. The blade was slightly blunt, his hair was thick. The way Hiten pulled at it hurt, but Jagmeet didn't say a word. He put up no defence, and feeling the man he loved behind him, so rough with him, he couldn't help it, he was getting hard.

Hiten turned him around and took out a razor blade. Jagmeet's beard wasn't long but it was still difficult to cut. Hiten spit in his hand and smeared it across Jagmeet's face. The blade ran cleaner through the wet hair, and Jagmeet hated how full of love he was, how much he liked the feeling of the metal on his skin, how much he wanted Hiten to continue. He knew he should have been resisting. But he wanted whatever Hiten wanted.

When he was done with the blade, Hiten pushed Jagmeet to his knees and put his cock in his mouth. He held what was left of Jagmeet's hair and controlled him. Then he pulled Jagmeet up and stripped him. Jagmeet turned. Hiten spat on himself, and then on him, and Jagmeet wanted it more than anything. Hiten pushed inside him and Jagmeet grunted. He said one word, 'yes', but Hiten told him to be quiet.

They took the backstreets home. When they met the main road, they spotted a mob. There were policemen among them, chanting along, 'khun badle ke khun.' Hiten stopped to look at Jagmeet, and then, without saying anything, ran off to join them. 'Khun badle ke khun,' he shouted. Those were the last words Jagmeet heard him say: '*blood for blood.*' Hiten led the group east down the road, which meant that Jagmeet could go west and make it home unseen. The house had been looted and trashed. It stank of piss. His father arrived not too long later.

'My son,' he said, seeing Jagmeet without his pagh, without his hair. 'My son.'

They sped out of the city; he'd never felt the wind like he did on the back of that motorbike. They drove until they had to stop for fuel. They pulled in at a dhaba by the side of the road, and his father started to fill the tank. There was the sound of howling in the distance, a horn beeping. The entrance to the dhaba opened and the owner shouted at them to get in.

'You can't leave the bike. They'll know.'

Jagmeet went inside while his father took the bike round to the back. The dhaba was empty, it was the middle of the night. Jagmeet realised the owner was Hindu. The shouting outside grew louder. A truck pulled in.

Jagmeet met his father in the kitchen. They hid in the ice box. The warmth of his father's body offset the cold meat and ice they lay on. When the owner finally opened the top, the light hurt Jagmeet's eyes.

'They're gone. It's safe.' His father headed straight for the door, but the owner grabbed his arm. 'Please. You must be hungry. Eat. It's all I can do.'

'We need to go.'

'Please.' He poured channa into two bowls and they ate.

They drove on into the farmland. He thought of the plans he'd made to run off and explore the world with Hiten. The plans to buy a farm far away, where no one knew them. For so long his image of happiness had taken such a certain shape, he couldn't imagine it in another form. He didn't want anything else. His future had been Hiten.

After a few months in Mata Ji's pindh, he was asked if he wanted to marry Amrit. He said yes, desperate to move forward away from his past, so that it could stay intact and unchanged.

The procession passed. Simran left the crowd to join Jagmeet and Aman. She had 'Never Forget' printed on her t-shirt. Jagmeet hugged her. They were almost out of food now, the imli water was warm and the filling had gone cold. He filled some puris for his daughters and one for him. He wondered what Amrit would have thought about them, *too much salt.* He missed her. He watched his daughters eat, smiling with their mouths full. He ate his one, the crisp puri shattering in one bite, the imli water shooting to each corner of his mouth at once.

Strange Attractor

—

'IF WE BELIEVE ONE EVENT CAUSES ANOTHER, free will cannot exist,' Kenny's ex said, before they split. 'I'm doing this because it's what I was always going to do.'

'The past is your context,' the clairvoyant said, a few weeks later. 'The present is your focus, and the future is your outcome. We can read them in any order.'

Kenny was keeping an open mind. His younger sister had brought him along, saying it would help with the break-up.

'It's less about the individual cards,' the clairvoyant continued, 'than the story they tell as one. Think, what thread ties the pictures together?'

Kenny turned over the past.

The tickets would expire in a week, the email said. Had it already been six months? He'd ordered two fast-track passes to Thorpe Park for his ex's birthday, an inside joke, but never got to use them. He thought going might bring closure, and he set off the next day, the only alone person in the theme park.

His ex was the thrill-seeker. But Kenny was enjoying himself, flying freely along different fixed tracks. He went on Oblivion twice, and his pass meant he waltzed right into Colossus. Coming out of the Nemesis Inferno gift shop, he paused at a kiosk selling ride photos to try and find himself. The images would make a nice little series, he thought. After seeing his photo, he glanced across the rest of the pictures and that was when he saw her, at the other end of the rollercoaster, a face he'd recognise anywhere: Raveena.

Raveena was the first and last life model he'd ever painted, excluding himself. Before her, Kenny solely painted strangers. For his

A-Level art project, he produced a series of studies of people on buses. And at university, he simply searched things like 'stock image person' or 'royalty free woman' and painted the results in a photorealist style. Despite harsh Crits, he doubled down on what he thought was his niche and began work on a series of computer-generated deepfakes – 'The Treachery of Images' for the meme age, etc – only for his tutor to suggest he work with a real person in the real world. He returned home for Christmas an artist unappreciated in his own time and opened the door to see Raveena.

She was his sister's GCSE maths tutor and studied Computer Science at a university near Kenny's. He walked her to the bus stop – it was late – and when he mentioned he was a painter, she looked up his Instagram right there. When he arrived home, he received a flurry of notifications: she'd liked all his work. In a moment of uncharacteristic bravery, he DMd her.

'Not to be weird but could I paint u sometime?'

'W clothes obvs,' he added.

'Sounds fun! Will check with bf :)'

How often can you just look at someone? When he painted her after his sister's maths lessons, Kenny felt an awkwardness that he had come to associate with intimacy. While he stared at her, and she looked off into the distance, his sister would watch, finishing her homework.

'Typical,' he remembered her saying. 'Talk about male gaze. Passive woman, active man.'

'I'm not passive,' Raveena said.

'You are here,' his sister said, standing behind his easel.

'Should I only paint men, then?' Kenny said, playing along.

'You want my honest opinion?' Not waiting for a response, she said, 'I think men should just stop for a few years. You've had, what, the entirety of history?'

When Raveena laughed, she laughed with her whole face.

'Like, you're literally turning her into a two-dimensional–'

'Am I all right to move?' Raveena asked Kenny. 'I've lost all feeling.'

Kenny looked away as she stretched.

In the photo at the kiosk, Raveena was sitting next to a man – a boyfriend? A husband?

A familiar jealousy stirred within Kenny. There were endless parallel universes in which he'd made a move back then and she'd ditched her boyfriend. There were infinite scenarios in which they could and would fall in love and here she was, in this world, reappearing in his life after all this time, and he was single.

In the four years since they last met, Kenny had seen Raveena twice. The first time, three years ago, he'd visited the offices of Henderson & Khan in Paddington's Little Venice to see his painting of her in the wild. The canvas was displayed in the waiting area, without its title. In the setting of the law firm, it was less a work of art than a piece of decoration – that, Kenny had thought, was its genius. Context was everything. The piece he'd based on a life model had itself become a kind of stock imagery.

In the painting, Raveena looks towards the viewer, but she avoids eye contact, doesn't return your gaze. If you were to approach the piece, you would find, with each step, that the realism of the representation gives way to something less defined, the person becoming shapes of colour, layers of paint. You start to see not only the brush strokes, but how the paint protrudes in some areas while others are so thin that the wash shows through. Take a step to the side and see how the glimmer of red in her inner eye stands out. Viewed from this angle, you couldn't possibly call it a tear duct, it's just paint, flaxseed oil blended with a pigment processed from scrap.

Kenny scanned the area around the kiosk for Raveena. People from his ride were still leaving the Nemesis Inferno gift shop. She

couldn't be far, but he worried that the moment might be missed
– there were so many people, she could have gone in any direction. There were thousands of scenarios in which he didn't find
her, but then he saw her, bent over, tying her shoelaces, near the
entrance to Angry Birds Land. Conscious of people looking at him
looking at her, he glanced away, and tried to find a place to stand
where she would see him. But she turned and walked off. He did
a half-run to get out ahead of her and, as if seeing her for the first
time, did a mime to communicate: *Raveena, is that you? Small world!*

Kenny had sent Raveena a photo of the piece when it was hung,
alongside his self-portrait, at his degree show – '*Diptych*, Kenneth
Cheung, Oil on Canvas'. She'd been unable to make it, off visiting the
boyfriend. Kenny didn't message her when it sold and because she
didn't know it had been bought, he never told her about the incident.

The facts of the incident were relayed to him by the Head
of Facilities at Henderson & Khan the second time he visited
the painting. A man who'd been prosecuted by one of the firm's
lawyers had come to reception intent on revenge. He smashed
a vase, spat at a security guard and punched a hole through the
canvas of Kenny's painting. It was torn right across Raveena's chest.
Kenny thought the company might commission another piece.

'I was thinking,' the Head of Facilities said, 'we could keep it up
as it is. As a kind of symbol. A constant reminder of what we do,
how our actions affect others. Powerful, no?'

Kenny didn't like how the story of the painting would eclipse
the piece itself. It was pretentious to keep it up, glib. 'You didn't get
it insured?' he asked.

'Small world!' he said, and she was the one to instigate the hug.

'This is Kenny,' Raveena said to the man next to her. 'He's an
artist.'

That was the word she used: artist.

'We're on a company away day, it's a whole thing,' she continued, and talked about her job. The man wasn't a boyfriend. He was a colleague. 'How about you?'

It dawned on Kenny how he must look to her: a grown man alone at a theme park. He could have told her the truth and she may or may not have felt sorry for him. He could have said that his friend – or partner? – had just gone to get food, but what if she saw him elsewhere in the park, alone again?

'Well, I was here with my friend,' he said. 'This is more his sort of thing. But he must have eaten something – he got sick after one of the rides and had to go home. I wanted to go with him, make sure he was okay, but he said it would be a waste of money. He was adamant.'

Raveena looked like she might be buying it. And then she asked – it was her who asked – whether he might like to join them. She wanted to go on Stealth, but her colleagues weren't feeling up to it. Kenny hadn't planned on trying the ride – it was the biggest one in the park and looked horrible – but he accepted with enthusiasm.

In the recent off-season, Stealth was disassembled and rebuilt with new parts. State-of-the-art sensors were installed, subject to rigorous checks. They came from the same factory, were built in the same batch and subject to the same conditions and yet one particular sensor malfunctioned, as it would always malfunction, at the exact time that Kenny and Raveena's carriage launched skywards. It triggered a safety warning, automatically engaging the emergency brakes at the top of the ride, stopping the rollercoaster just before its sixty-metre drop, suspending Kenny, Raveena and all the other passengers high above the park.

Dark spots appeared over the bird's-eye view of the theme park. The wind cut cold. A crowd gathered below. In the afternoon's dying light, Kenny made out the faint glimmer of camera flashes.

'Please do not panic,' the loudspeaker repeated, 'help is on its way.'

Kenny was showing no external signs of panic. He didn't want to seem afraid in front of Raveena. There was nothing to do but wait.

Her eyes were shut, so he looked at her. The man behind them had stopped hyper-ventilating. The teenagers at the back were still singing that Sketch song, 'Waiting for the Drop Like'. Birds flew beneath them. He noticed how quickly the clouds were moving. A light rain began to fall, despite the clear forecast.

After ten minutes, a drone appeared and circled the carriage. It was carrying a camera that recorded footage that was later included in a YouTube compilation, 'Epic Rollercoaster Fails II', which Kenny showed to countless people over the years.

'That's really you, there?' his niece said, a decade later.

'Yes,' Kenny said. 'That's really me.'

'Were you scared?'

'Of course. Terrified. I thought, "This is it."'

They were on their way to the Science Museum. Kenny's job was to keep his niece entertained for the day. His sister's C-section was scheduled for that afternoon, and soon his niece would have a baby brother.

He paused the video, seeing Raveena. When he remembered her in the seat next to him, it was from the viewpoint of the drone, slowly zooming out. This wasn't a world in which they fell in love. But there were so many worlds in which they'd never met, so many where they'd never existed.

The park's engineers had taken the passengers down the ladder one by one. The rungs were slick and cold with rain. The ladder led to a cherry picker, which slowly lowered him to the cheering crowd. Raveena had waited for him below. He hugged her. They walked out of the park together, accompanied by her colleagues, and then branched off in separate directions to find their cars.

Kenny and his niece arrived at the museum. They looked at rockets and planets and robots. Still thinking of Raveena, he googled Henderson & Khan and found out that the firm no longer existed. No one had let him know what had become of the painting. He wasn't sure if it was the painting that he missed, or Raveena, or the image of Raveena that the painting had solidified, or the person he'd been when he made the painting, a person with so many paths open to him, of which he'd only been able to take one.

Kenny was tired and his niece was getting irritable. He was tempted to cut the visit short when they came across an exhibit called 'The Shape of Chaos' which contained a series of visualisations – prints and 3D models – of strange attractors. A quote was projected onto the first wall:

> We may regard the present state of the universe as the effect of its past and the cause of its future. An intellect which at a certain moment would know all forces that set nature in motion, and all positions of all items of which nature is composed; if this intellect were also vast enough to submit these data to analysis it would embrace in a single formula the movements of the greatest bodies of the universe and those of the tiniest atom; for such an intellect nothing would be uncertain and the future just like the past would be present before its eyes.
>
> Pierre Simon Laplace

In the first room there was a double pendulum. His niece set it in motion, and the arm of the device danced with no conceivable pattern or rhythm, before losing momentum and coming to a standstill. On the wall there was a 2D phase space visualisation of the pendulum, where every possible state of the object was plotted onto a graph. The double pendulum, the caption read, could be used as a model for understanding chaos theory; you can never release it and make it behave the same way twice, and yet, all its possible positions, all its possible futures, are fixed. 'Chaos,' the caption read, 'is sensitive dependence on initial conditions.' The smallest change in input can cause a significant difference in output. A chaotic system is both deterministic and completely unpredictable. In one room a GIF visualisation of something called 'The Logistic Map' played on repeat, but Kenny didn't pause to read about it. In the next room, videos of weather patterns played on small screens, opposite a sculpture called 'Lorenz Attractor in X–Z Phase Plane'. 'Locally unstable and globally stable,' the video voice-over said, 'no matter what the start-point is, a chaotic system will always evolve into a state on the strange attractor.'

Kenny googled strange attractor: 'an equation or fractal set representing a complex pattern of behaviour in a chaotic system … Any two arbitrarily close initial points on the attractor are arbitrarily far apart within a different iteration on the attractor.' He couldn't understand any of it. He put his phone away and looked at the work. His niece pointed at the different images:
   'Bird.'
   'Racetrack.'
   'Ball of yarn.'

A video played at the end of the exhibition. It was an infinite zoom into a Mandelbrot set with another voice-over:

> 'Life as we know it is governed by deterministic chaos. There's a pattern in all things, but on a scale of complexity that we cannot perceive. For the history of humanity, we have derived meaning by looking back at events and making connections and patterns. Who knows, maybe with the processing power of future generations of super-computers, we might be able to map chaotic systems with greater accuracy and turn our gaze forwards.'

In the gift shop, Kenny bought his niece a set of bouncy balls that looked like the planets of the solar system. He checked his phone again, a little worried at the lack of news and called his brother-in-law, who didn't pick up. Unsure what to do, he decided to head back. On the train, his niece wanted to play Guess-What. He found different images on his phone and zoomed in so far that they became abstract shapes. Then his niece had to guess what they were.

'Apple.'

'Tree.'

'Mummy.'

In the first month after his nephew's birth, Kenny's sister rested. His brother-in-law looked after the kids and Kenny came round to help cook and clean. His sister wanted to do things the way their parents and grandparents would have liked and gave Kenny a book of confinement recipes to cook from. Kenny couldn't remember their parents ever talking about zuo yuezi but went along with it. Taking a fish soup up to her room, he found her on her phone, swiping away.

'I really think it's time you sort through your stuff,' she said.

His boxes in the attic had been untouched since Dad passed. He kept a few of his old Transformers for his niece and put the rest of the stuff in big bags. When he was done, he found, knew he would find, the self-portrait he'd completed for his degree show, all those years ago, one half of 'Diptych'. There wasn't a single good thing to do with a self-portrait. It's not like he could gift it to someone. And he certainly couldn't put it up in his own place. But to bin one of his last remaining works?

When she'd finished sitting the month, Kenny drove his sister and his niece to the supermarket.

'First time out the house in weeks and you're on your phone?' Kenny said.

'You really are turning into Dad,' his sister said.

His niece started to act up inside. When her mum wouldn't buy her the cereal she wanted, she threw three of her bouncy balls down the aisle. Kenny found Earth and Jupiter but couldn't find Saturn. He had a horrible feeling that someone might slip and fall on the missing ball. Could his niece not getting Coco Pops cause someone to break their arm? His sister and niece carried on shopping while he looked. But it was well and truly gone. He made the decision to leave it.

In the car, his sister shrieked.

'You've got a match!'

'Excuse me?'

'I got you a match.'

She showed him her phone, an image of a smiling woman on a dating app.

'You can't be serious.'

'What do you want me to say to her?'

'Do you realise how tragic this makes me feel?'

'Should we play it cool, just like, "hey"?'

'I don't need–'

'Like, "Hey, I'm new to this. How are you doing?"'

'Don't say that. Give me the phone. What photo did you use?'

'She seems really cool,' she said, and showed the phone to her daughter in the back. 'What do you think, pretty right? Good for Uncle Kenny?'

Full of nervous energy before his date, Kenny sanded down the canvas, flattening the surface of his self-portrait. Then he covered it with white paint and put it up for free collection online.

The canvas was picked up by a market artist. She used it for a vanitas still life: bowl of fruit about to rot, flowers on the edge of wilting, etc. The piece was bought by a couple visiting London on their honeymoon, and taken back to Glasgow, where it stayed in their guest bedroom until their grandson came to visit and spotted some faint marks showing through the thinning paint. The grandson posted a photo online, where it caught the attention of an artist who was working on a series called 'Pentimenti'. The artist bought the piece for much more than the couple thought it was worth and produced an X-ray scan of the canvas, which showed ghostly white traces of the original painting beneath, the image distorted by noise like an ultrasound. A collection of the artist's scans was displayed at a small but prestigious East London gallery to relative critical success. While the 'original' scans sold for four-figure sums, copies were available to visitors at cost. 'Still Life/Self-Portrait' was hung at the end of the exhibition, which you approach down a long hallway. From one end of the hall, it looks like an abstract piece, with no determinable pattern to the white marks on black, but as you near it, a face begins to emerge, he's looking right at you.

Flight Path

—

PRITI HADN'T FINISHED THE HURRICANE. It sat on the window-sill where Mum had left it, still without its propellor. Priti had read the instructions cover to cover, knew that the nose and the body connected through piece forty-two. But it was always Mum that finished the planes.

Their fleet started with the Spitfire. Priti had spotted it at the RAF museum gift shop, and that was that. It was Priti's job to read the instructions. Mum would sit on the floor and get frustrated with the small pieces.

Priti took the remaining parts of the Hurricane out of the box. She picked up a propeller blade. It was the colour of bone. She put it in her mouth. Ms McCarthy said plastic lives forever. In the future, aliens would discover her planes and piece them together like the dinosaurs at the Natural History Museum. She'd seen them in real life, the dinosaurs, though the skeletons were out of reach. In one room, her mum let her touch the mammoth. Its fur felt like coconut. Then a guard came over, and Mum pretended not to speak English. She talked away in Punjabi and they rushed out of the museum, laughing. But on the underground, Priti was asking too many questions, and Mum asked for Statue Time. She didn't budge. In her head she was an exhibit in a future alien museum. *This is a human*, the sign next to her would say, in an alien language. *They walked the Earth on two legs.*

She spat out the blade and put it back in the box. It was shiny with saliva. Ms McCarthy said saliva breaks food down. They'd watched a video in Science of a bird throwing up food into its baby's mouth. Mum hadn't even known what regurgitate meant. Nani definitely wouldn't know. She was singing in the kitchen. Mum said Nani was sharp and couldn't keep time.

'Nani, you're sharp and can't keep time,' Priti told Nani that night, as she sang 'sonja bai' to her in bed. She smiled and carried on singing. Nani sang to her every night, even now she was eight. Priti pretended to sleep.

*

Seeing her little rani so soothed by her voice made Nani smile. She looked down at her granddaughter and remembered singing the same lullaby to her daughter, Priti's mother. It was a lullaby she remembered from when she was a child, lying in her own mother's lap. As she stroked Priti's hair, Nani thought of that childhood home in Punjab, and in her head she walked from room to room, up the stairs, running from roof to roof, chased by her brother, shouted at by neighbours, who, playing cards or opening pea pods, huddled in the shade of hung washing. There was another family in that house now, those rooms held someone else's memories.

*

When Nani finally left, Priti flipped open Mum's phone. She clicked through the gallery, opening the last photo they'd taken together, Mum dressed up for a night out, her hair dyed blue, and Priti making a face. Then she loaded Asteroids and, level by level, slipped into sleep.

'One!' Priti said, as they left for school in the morning, pointing up to the first plane of the day.
     'Why no Punjabi, rani?' Nani asked, as always.
     'Why no English, Nani?' Priti said, bobbing her head like Apu.
     '...'
     'Two!'
Priti liked living on the flight path. She liked to count the planes in the sky, praying no one went to the loo. Fatima said that when you poo on a plane and flush, it drops straight out the bottom. Priti imagined walking to school one day and getting hit. But she had it

figured out – if the plane was above her, it meant that it was near the airport, close to landing or take-off, which meant the seatbelt signs would be on, and no one could go to the toilet. This was the safest place to be.

'Three.'

*

Nani sighed as another plane passed. Priti started saying something. Nani smiled and nodded, not understanding. It sounded like something to do with toilets. They'd only just left the house. Priti was saying something else. Nani's English was bad, Priti's Punjabi worse. At first, they couldn't talk at all without Priti's mum around to translate. But little by little, they made do. Nani learnt the words for *eat your food* and *we're running late*. Priti learnt to say *I don't know* in three different ways.

'Four.'

*

Nani was saying something. They cut across the grass, dew squeaking beneath their shoes. The walk was long, but Nani still wouldn't let her on the bus. 'No car, no bus, rani,' she'd say. No ifs, no buts. 'Bas' meant 'stop' in Punjabi, Priti knew that much. 'Bas kar' meant 'stop that'. She heard that a lot. Bas kar, bus, car. Stop that bus. Car. Stop.

They crossed onto the path and Nani went back to whatever it was she was saying. Something about cars, or keys – car keys? Or lunch. While she talked, the possibilities grew in Priti's head: Nani had put extra in her lunch money for sweets, or she'd been able to sell what was left of Mum's car, or she wasn't going to be able to pick Priti up today so–

'Fucking pakis.' A cyclist swerved past and stopped a few metres ahead. 'Can't you read? Cycle. Lane.'

He spat on the path and sped off. Priti imagined the saliva breaking the ground. Nani didn't speak until the school gates. Priti carried on counting planes, but in her head.

At playtime, Priti and Fatima made paper planes out of their French quizzes. They stood on the roots of the willow at the edge of the playground and let loose, aiming for the sun.

'Mine can fly backwards,' Fatima said.

'Mine's a Boeing 747. It has 660 seats.'

Priti knew all about 747s, she'd been on one when she went with Mum and Nani to Punjab. It was her first time, and she'd printed off the Wikipedia page about the plane. It was just like the photos. There were stairs *inside*. India, though, was not what she'd had in mind. When they landed, there were no elephants basking in the sun. Monsoon season had just begun, and cars waded through the flooded streets.

Mum's hair was black for the first time in ages. They spent the whole holiday visiting people. Priti's cousins found it funny that she couldn't understand them; she was sure, when they spoke, that they were making fun of her. When the adults asked why Priti didn't speak, her mum answered for her. Nani, on the other hand, didn't stop talking. Wherever they went, their relatives gathered around her like she was famous. She made them all laugh with different stories and jokes that Priti pretended to understand.

On the plane back – a 720 – Nani stared quietly at the home screen in front of her while Priti and her mum watched cartoons. Priti wasn't even scared when there was turbulence. At Heathrow, Nani asked Priti a question. Mum translated: 'How did you like it?'

'I love flying.'

Mum translated this back, but what she said was longer.

Nani said something else.

'She says you'll have to visit lots when she moves back.'

*

74

While Priti was at school, Nani watched cartoons.

'I love muddy pudders,' she said, along with Peppa. She paused. 'I love muddy puddles. Puddles.'

She'd wanted to know English ever since she was a child. Her brother's school taught it, and each evening, she'd watch him do his homework. He promised to tutor her: 'Say fuck. Say shit.'

It wasn't fair, he didn't even like school. He dropped out as soon as he was old enough to drive a taxi. In the months she spent waiting for her visa, she rode around in her brother's cab, listening to English lessons on cassettes. Sitting in the passenger seat as he drove around Ludhiana, she imagined London. 'Thank you, Sir. Thank you, Madame,' she recited. When she finally had her ticket, her brother drove her to Delhi, her parents quiet in the back. On the plane, she craned her neck to see the ever-shrinking cars below, trying to guess which one was his.

'Thank you,' she said to her husband, getting into his car. She expected him to want to speak English, but he seemed so happy to be able to talk to someone in Punjabi, so eager to chat after long shifts of conveyor belt silence, that she stopped trying to speak English at home. She got a job at the airport and expected to have to learn. But all the other cleaners were immigrants too, and, in the middle of the night, as they glided across the vast halls of Departures, not a word of English could be heard.

Now, a lifetime later, she watched cartoons with determination. She imagined watching TV with Priti, laughing together at the same jokes. She squinted at the screen, trying to concentrate, the edges of her vision a dark blur. This shrinking of her sight had started when her daughter died, or at least, that's when she first noticed it. She thought it was the grief, that the darkness she felt within was seeping into her eyes, onto the world; whenever she saw something, she was made aware of a visible absence, her periphery obscured. She struggled, now, to take in the whole TV. Peppa she could see, but the other pigs were fading. The show ended.

'Go compare! Go compare!'

The ads always reminded Nani of her daughter. She could recite most adverts line by line, would hum every jingle. She'd had such a good memory, and Nani had enjoyed nothing more than to sit with her and reminisce, her daughter telling her about that time they got lost in Wolverhampton and ended up at the wrong Gurd- wara, sitting through a stranger's Sukhmani Sahib, or the time they got that flat on the M1 and the two of them changed the tyre, or when she took Nani out for her first ever cappuccino, her first ever croissant. Her daughter had never forgotten a face, or a name, or a birthday. It was impossible to know just how much had been lost.

Nani enjoyed having the house to herself when her grand- daughter was at school. For Priti, she spent so much energy trying to seem like she had everything under control. But she didn't want to be okay. Certain things you shouldn't move past. At times, she felt almost resentful of Priti, felt she'd somehow been robbed of her own grief. How could the child ever be happy if her grandmother was forever sad? A few weeks back, when Priti wet the bed again, Nani found herself full of anger cleaning the sheets, getting Priti in the shower. She'd been up late finalising the sale of the house that she was supposed to spend her retirement in, had to do it all over the phone, not even getting one last trip. It was supposed to be passed down to her daughter and then to Priti, but here it was disappearing in the dark, so that she could afford to raise her grand- daughter. The girl was crying, and Nani wanted so badly to join in, to let it all go. But she dried Priti off, brushed her hair and plaited it for school. 'Okay. It's okay. Bas. We're running late.'

'Don't delay,' the next advert said. 'Claim today.'

She heard the letterbox open and close. The letter was from the hospital; she knew 'NHS'. She could read the date and her name but not much else. She folded it and put it in her bag, noticing the time. She was supposed to have cleaned before picking up Priti. She pulled the Henry Hoover around the house, ending in her granddaughter's room. She went over the carpet, watching the nozzle disappear into the dark edges. She imagined the blurring as a layer of dust framing her eyes, imagined the hoover cleaning it all up, sucking whatever it was out of her, the world returning clear and full.

She heard the crash before she saw it, one of Priti's boxes on the floor, little pieces across the carpet.

'Fuck. Shit.'

Ms McCarthy's class was late to let out at home-time. The sun was out, and Nani was wearing her favourite suit, the pink one with the flowers. The other parents talked at the gates. Nani remembered picking her daughter up from the same school decades ago. Not that she picked her up often, normally sleeping through the afternoons ahead of her night shift. Seeing how her daughter was with Priti, all those years later, always playing games with her, taking her out, Nani realised that she hadn't been much of a mother herself. She used to have selfish thoughts, sometimes fantasising about a life alone. During her shifts, she dreamed up a vision of retirement, moving back to the house in Punjab, a manja in the shade. But here she was, in grey London, doing it all again. Hard not to think her life was repeating itself as Priti left her classroom – the girl was a carbon copy of her mother. Before the ridiculous hair, before the useless boy.

*

As Priti left 4C, her heart sank. Nani had on Mum's old trainers, the Reeboks. Bright green with *that* suit! Priti tried to rush over before the other girls saw, but Ms McCarthy called Nani over for a chat. While her teacher talked at Nani, Priti looked at the hair on Nani's arms. She wished she would get rid of it.

'Do you understand?' Ms McCarthy said.

'Thank you, Madame.'

Ms McCarthy asked Ms Khan to translate. Ms Khan talked in Urdu and Nani responded in Punjabi. Priti pulled a piece of paper out of Nani's handbag. It had her real name on it, a name Priti had never heard out loud. She read the letter in her head. Glaucoma. She tried to split up the sounds. She knew a coma was sleeping for a long time.

'I think she got the general gist,' Ms Khan said.

Priti continued to read the letter. Was Nani entering a coma? She imagined having to visit her at the hospital, her body a statue. In the shows Mum liked, people always came out of comas and remembered nothing. Maybe Nani would return happy, cracking jokes again.

Priti folded the letter, making a Concorde, long and thin. Ms McCarthy called Gujan's mum over from the gates. Gujan and his mum spoke Punjabi to each other, even though they both knew English.

'Could you say that tomorrow we're doing our time capsule assembly?'

Gujan's mum smiled at Nani and started talking in Punjabi. Ms McCarthy continued. 'The kids need to bring something special to go in the capsule. And to practise public speaking, they're to give a speech. Every year we ask the parents and guardians ...'

Priti threw the plane, but it didn't go far. She couldn't keep up with the conversation. Next to Punjabi, even English sounded foreign. Ms McCarthy said something, then Gujan's mum, then Nani, then Gujan's mum and so on. It was like they were playing pass the parcel, unwrapping another sentence each time it went round. It ended with Nani, and the two of them walked home through the park, looking both ways.

It didn't take Priti long to realise that piece forty-two was missing. Without it, the propeller would never attach. Without the propeller there was no plane and the fleet would be incomplete forever.

*

Priti tore through the house, lifting everything she could. She kept shouting words that Nani didn't know. Nani had no idea what she was looking for. When Priti showed her the plane and the box, Nani rushed to her bedroom. Nothing under the bed. Nothing behind the chest of drawers. She explained what might have happened to Priti.

'I don't know what you're saying. Say it normal or don't say anything!'

'Bas kar,' Nani shouted, not wanting to be angry.

Priti made a point of storming off, almost tripping over the hoover.

*

Priti couldn't sleep. She didn't want Mum's phone or TV. She wanted to sit with Mum and play Air Traffic Control. She listened to the sirens outside, her room flashing blue. She thought about all the times Mum lost things, usually her keys. The last time, she was late for a party and frantically retracing her steps around the house. Panting, she came into Priti's room, 'Bug, you seen Mum's keys?'

Priti helped her look, and it became a game. They ran around the house shouting: 'Not by the door,' 'Not under the sofa,' 'Not in the bath.' It was Priti who finally found them – in the fridge! She ran to her mum and placed the cold metal in her palm.

*

Nani ran her fingers over Henry's head, trying to figure out how to open the thing. It had always been her daughter's job to hoover; the last thing Nani wanted after a shift at the airport, or the hotel, was more cleaning. She found the latch and slowly emptied the bag onto the kitchen floor.

Amongst the dust was all sorts, but mostly hair. Long strands of

Priti's hair were intertwined with Nani's white, wiry knots. And in the mess on the floor, Nani found some of the different-coloured strands of her daughter's hair.

Her daughter's friend owned a salon on the parade down the road. When Nani was watching Priti, she'd go for a few hours and return looking like a different person. The dying had started off years before as an act of rebellion, a call for attention. But when her daughter moved back home with a daughter of her own and no husband, Nani barely noticed the changing colours.

By the time you got used to the silver, it would be purple and cropped. Nani was only ever shocked when it was black as the day she was born. She could remember it so clearly; everyone who'd visited the hospital marvelled at her full head of hair. The morticians had dyed it black for the funeral. When she saw it, she wished she'd told them to leave it as her daughter had wanted it. Dark green, or was it blue?

She put some of the strands to one side. Humming the Peppa Pig theme tune, she sifted through the rest of the dust, picking out objects: the odd screw, a few coins. LEGO, popcorn kernels, pistachio shells, the little crescents of cut nails, small shards of glass. And finally, nestled in a Starburst wrapper, she saw it, the missing piece.

She binned the dust and rubbish but hoovered up the hair. She washed her ashy fingers with Fairy and went to Priti's room.

'Nani Ji!

Priti hugged her tight. She got her to sit on the floor with her. She pointed to the instructions and chatted away. Nani smiled and nodded. She could make out certain words, but by the time she pieced them together, Priti was on to something else.

*

Priti read the instructions one final time. Nani sang and stroked her hair. The propeller slipped into place. She spun the blades. The aliens of the future would marvel. She showed it to Nani.

'All right! Priti for the win,' Nani said in English, quoting a cartoon.

'Nani, how do you say thank you in Punjabi?'

'Sorry?' Nani asked, smiling slightly.

Nani sat next to Gujan's mum at the show and tell assembly. She was wearing normal shoes. They were talking, and Gujan's mum was laughing.

Priti span the propellers, waiting. Fatima had brought a Bratz doll, and Gujan a Yu-Gi-Oh shiny. When it was their turn, they had to talk about their object, and why they wanted it to be put in the capsule. Priti's name was called, and she went up to the stage.

*

When Priti finished speaking, she put the toy plane in the box. Nani asked Kaz, Gujan's mum, to translate for her.

When the assembly was over, Kaz told Nani how Gujan had lost the book he was supposed to put in the time capsule. He phoned her from school, asking if she could go home and look for it, but she couldn't just leave work.

'Now I'm the world's worst mum,' she said. 'Because he had nothing on him to give except his favourite card.'

'He's like me. I lose everything,' Nani said. 'I got a letter yesterday afternoon, and by the evening I had no idea where it was. Not a clue!'

They followed everyone outside. Someone had dug a hole near the giant willow. The teacher lowered the box into the ground and covered it with dirt.

Afterwards, Kaz and Nani took Priti, Fatima and Gujan to the park. The sun had turned up, bringing along its joggers and buggies.

The grass was patchworked with picnic blankets, balloon-sized bubbles and barbecue smoke filled the air. 'Greensleeves' played on repeat from the Mr Whippy.

'Can we? Please?'

The kids ran off, coins clenched in tight fists. They darted past a vendor selling scoobies, and around a group of men playing cricket, using a tree trunk for wickets. Someone was playing bhangra from a stereo and Priti sang along, making up the words.

Nani and Kaz found a bench and talked. Once Nani got started, there was no stopping her. She could talk for England as long as it wasn't in English, her daughter used to say. She told Kaz about her pindh, had she heard of it? And if so, did she know so-and-so from such-and-such? The questioning continued until they found some common link, an uncle of Kaz's who might have been a teacher at the school Nani's brother had gone to all those years ago.

'Oh, look at them,' Kaz said, spotting the children at the top of the climbing frame. They sat, dangling their legs between the ropes, watching two other kids hanging upside down from the monkey bars, on opposite ends, swinging and swinging, with their arms outstretched, inches from touching.

After planning the next playdate, Gujan and his mum left with Fatima. The park slowly emptied. Priti lay next to Nani on the grass. Nani stroked her long black hair and started to sing, softly, 'Sonja bai, sonja bai.' Priti, tired from all the running, drifted off. The sun set, the grass grew cold. Nani replayed the day in her head, committing it to memory. She looked up at the sky and she started to see the stars. She could still remember some of the constellations her mother had taught her. Out of the edges of her vision, the blinking light of an airplane emerged, joining the dots between the stars, before disappearing again. Nani wondered where it was headed. She thought of all the people on it, looking down at this shrinking park, out at the city, the endless red and white lights of cars heading home or venturing out – the plane rising, levelling above the clouds. As the view vanished, she thought of them pulling down their window shades and turning back to the screens in front of them, tracking their own small progress across the pixelated map.

'One!' Nani said, waking Priti up, and they walked home, counting out loud.

SYM

—

WAY BACK WHEN, Jat was an untouchable raider, light on his feet, not built like the lads these days, who made his son roll his eyes as they took off their shirts to oil up. The boy used to be game, would play matches with Jat in the back garden, going blue in the face, out of breath, but now he just went through the motions, humouring his old man, wanting to be elsewhere and giving Jat a look as he took another swig of Jameson's as if it wasn't a free country. Jat had been bringing the kid since the tournaments began and each year the crowds got bigger, there were even goreh watching now, imagine, men who were boys throwing stones at Jat and his mates as they played, his breath in those days endless: kabaddi kabaddi kabaddi until white mums picketed the school gates and apneh had to get bussed out the borough, long coach rides to a school which was all goreh, which was fights every break, whites spitting in his lunch, lines in detention – I will not speak Punjabi in class, I will not speak – detention making him miss the safe coach home, long walks down the Broadway doing his best to dodge the paki-bashers, some days not trying that hard, part of him wanting to get jumped, part of him asking for it, wanting to have at them, front jab smashing glasses, uppercut forcing teeth into tongue, turning white red, wanting to hit and be hit, to break up long days with nothing to do, none of his old mates up for kabaddi, either working now at factories and shops, or shut in by parents too scared to let them out, scarred by stories of kids getting carved up with Stanley knives by the National Front, stories of the body found outside the Dominion, 18, only 18, and then the teacher offed in broad daylight by pigs at the protest. Jat had to get inventive to get a game together, ended up joining the Southall Youth Movement on Featherstone to get enough numbers for teams. They'd head down to Southall Park and Jat would hold his breath and run. Once or twice teddy boys tried to start something, and they got back what they gave to put it nice, which surprised Jat, these

SYM lads into their politics and all. Whenever he turned up at the house, they'd be reading books or 'having discussions', freshie music on in the background. This one time, in 81, he arrived, and they were playing punk not bhangra, having heard that a Nazi band called the 4-Skins had been booked to play the Hambrough, and would be bringing their Nazi fans to Southall. They asked the pub to cancel. Asked the police to intervene. Only option left was to turn up and send a message. The coaches arrived: Nazi salutes, paki-chants, the works, was even a guy who had his trousers down and his pale arse pressed up to the window, these were the people the police had showed up to protect, punks spilling into the pub already pissed off their heads. There was talk in the crowd that they'd already made a pit stop to trash the Maharaja Cash and Carry, clear now, if it wasn't already, that they weren't here for music. The police looked on as a couple of skinheads turned on two women passing on the pavement. That, for Jat, was it. He wanted to kill, wanted to beat, stab and strangle – they charged and the police, surprise, surprise, tried to protect the skinheads; for all Jat knew, one of these bastards was the copper that murdered the teacher, one of these bastards stormed People Unite, rode his horse into the peaceful sit-in, one of these pigs hit Harp's mum with a truncheon, these were the fuckers who turned a blind eye to blood in the streets, who saw the body of the boy on the railings and did nothing, who did everything to defend the National Front on St George's Day, to defend Nazis today. It ended now, had to end, him and his kabaddi mates breaking down the wall by Ruskin Road and lobbing bricks, Jat praying one of his might hit one of these mohawked freaks; he wanted to see blood, to make blood, threw brick after brick for the spat-on kids, the carved-up backs, for the broken-in houses, the swastikas on doors, for the dog shit in his locker, for every hit he took that day behind the sheds – he wanted to get closer, to throw punches, but what must have been a Molotov hit the Hambrough and set the pub up in flames, a proper fire, the real thing, the burning sending the skinheads off running: men who would be fathers who would be grandfathers, and the police charging: men who would be fathers who would be grandfathers. Jat turned and ran, trying to control his breath as he passed St George's, taking Greenford and Shackleton onto Lady Margaret, the air running thin and his throat burning kabaddi kabaddi kabaddi kabaddi kabaddi

The Turn

—

1

'THE FUTURE ISN'T RENEWABLE,' the journalist said. 'There's science and then there's common sense.'

The presenter, who died last year, asked a question.

Sol, feet up on the coffee table, dipped his biscuit in his tea, and Trish, watching from the kitchen, willed it to break and fall. He'd only boiled enough for one cup.

Trish filled the kettle. One of them received a message. They had identical text alerts, the same phones. She remembered that day at Westfield, playing on the iPads with Jenny at Apple, and Sol surprising them: three brand new phones. In those days, Trish knew better than to ask where the money had come from.

The experts on the TV continued arguing. Trish wished they hadn't gone open plan. She checked her phone: no messages. She went back to the kitchen table, where there were vendors to set up, POs to process. She looked over at her husband, 'I don't know why she doesn't call.'

He paused the debate. 'Who, Jenny? She texted earlier.'

'You talked and you didn't tell me?'

'Talked, we didn't talk. It was a text.'

'How is she?'

'She's good.'

'What did she say?'

'That she's good.'

'Why can't she just use the group?'

Trish tried to get back to work but was easily distracted with Sol home. The endless text alerts, discussions on the news, a tennis ball landing in their garden from next door, bright green on the dull lawn. She checked Jenny's Instagram. No new posts, though she didn't post often. You only had to scroll a few rows to see the photo of the two of them at the peak of Ben Nevis, the last summer before she left.

She remembered that long drive, Jenny playing Sketch's *The Rapture* on repeat. The path up the mountain had been quiet, the wind making waves in the tall grass. Her fondest memories were in nature with her daughter. Sol didn't get it, driving hours only to walk in the rain carrying a child who wouldn't remember a thing. When Jenny was old enough to walk without help, Sol stopped coming on the trips and it became their time, the hiking, and with those long stretches without seeing anyone, it really felt like it could be just the two of them on the mountain, the whole valley theirs.

She wanted to chat with Jenny. She found a GIF of a cartoon plane skywriting 'missing you'. She watched it repeat a few times and then deleted it. She typed: 'loving the new Sketch album – have u heard?'

She sent it and clicked back into her messages. Under Jenny was a message from West London Monumental Masonry. It was a week old now and Trish was yet to reply.

West London Monumental Masonry was Tayo. He ran the account – it was his business – occasionally posting (as tastefully as possible) new additions to the extensive range of headstones he provided. She'd visited his studio a few weeks ago, works in progress held in vices: Lenuta Văduvă, Paddy McCarthy.

'Have you ever made a spelling mistake on one?'

'Everyone asks that. Why does everyone ask that?'

She watched him work for a few minutes. How ridiculous her desire seemed to her, how adolescent. She wondered if either of them would have been attracted to each other if they hadn't known one another as teenagers, bored at the currency exchange. She wanted to feel guilty for wanting him, tried to think of Sol and Jenny.

She understood the undercurrents of her desire. Tayo was the path not taken, the fork in the road. Being with him might allow her to see the life she could have had, the person she could have been. Unfortunately, analysing the desire didn't stop her feeling it.

At 19, Trish and Tayo used to get the same bus to and from Heathrow. Their manager at the currency exchange would split them up when they arrived. He didn't think it looked good if they both worked the till at the same time. They looked forward to days when they could work together in the back. Tayo loved to pose with the stacks of cash, and, on multiple occasions, had made it rain. He was a boy in a man's body, and Trish was old enough to know what she wanted. She wanted a man like Sol, who met them for lunch most days, a book in the pocket of his jacket. Sol talked slowly about politics and history. He was calm and measured about everything – except the NBA.

After she got her first accountancy job and Sol got his position in air-traffic control, they got married and Tayo exited the stage like so many people in her life would. But then Jenny finally set Trish up on social media and there he was. She surprised herself with how much she wanted to meet him.

'Sol as in Sol Sol?' he said.

'Yeah. Almost twenty-five years.'

'Kids?'

'A daughter.'

'Man, Sol. You know what he called me once? A human dumbbell.'

She laughed.

'I can hardly remember those days. But I remember that name.'

They weren't doing anything wrong, but Trish asked that they talk on Instagram and not on the Facebook account that Sol sometimes used. They talked on and off for a while. He wasn't a very good texter. They agreed to meet in person. She invited him over for lunch. She had the house to herself during the days – she worked from home, Sol worked at Heathrow, Jenny had moved out.

She didn't know what to cook. She didn't want it to seem like she'd made too much effort, but she did want to impress him. Which was also why she'd tried on three different outfits. Everything seemed to send the wrong message. But what did she want to say? She cleaned the house, not that he'd notice. She put the family photos in the cupboard, not wanting to catch Sol's eye when they did what they were going to do – what were they going to do? What on earth was she doing? Maybe he wouldn't expect anything. It was just two old friends meeting up. Lunch. She poured herself a glass of wine, turning off the news that had been on since Sol left for work.

She let Tayo in. He smelled like aftershave. She realised she wasn't wearing perfume. She poured him a drink and excused herself. Upstairs, she put on her Chanel and took a moment to reset. She hadn't felt this insecure in years, but what use was security? Security was watching TV with Sol, calling the Paper Lantern and reciting the numbers of their Friday night takeout order by heart. On the rare occasions when they did have sex, they'd follow the same sequence of positions, the two of them quiet even after Jenny moved out. Sometimes Trish would try something new, and Sol would be game, but still, he could only ever finish the same certain way. A few weeks ago, there was a sex scene in the film they were watching, and Sol automatically changed the channel to the news, like he used to when Jenny was with them. He'd been a different man ever since starting Group. Which was a good thing, she knew, but she missed those nights when he'd come home having hit big, filled with energy and desire.

She headed back down and plated up the food. They talked about the old days, about their manager, the customers. Tayo had married not long after Trish and divorced a few years ago.

'Best decision I ever made,' he said.

Trish laughed.

The doorbell rang.

The doorbell rang again.

'I – should I, like, hide?' he said.

'If it was Sol he'd use his key,' she said.

A knock at the door. Trish's phone rang: Jenny.

'You smell nice,' Jenny said, as they hugged. 'I thought I'd surprise you. I missed you.'

'I missed you, too,' Trish said, and then paused. 'We were just having lunch. I'll make you a plate.' She took a deep breath and walked through to the kitchen. 'Jenny, Tayo. Tayo, Jenny.'

'Early for wine,' Jenny said.

Trish tried to keep a level head. They were two friends having lunch. They hadn't even touched each other. Those were the facts.

'It's five o'clock somewhere,' Tayo said. 'You want some?'

There was nothing that Jenny could suspect. They ate, shared stories. She saw Tayo off at the door. She'd avoided something reckless, and no one was any the wiser. When she returned, Jenny was on her phone, and the family photos that she had hidden were back in their places.

Jenny had viewed her message. Trish watched the little dots as she typed. She hadn't talked to Tayo since the visit. It was the last time she'd seen him or Jenny. Lockdown started a week later. With flights grounded, Sol was put on furlough, and here they were, spending more time than they ever had together.

Jenny heart-reacted to her message. Trish waited for an actual reply. She answered an email about an upcoming meeting, then checked her phone again. Nothing. Just a little heart next to her message – that wasn't a reply, this wasn't a conversation.

Another tennis ball landed in their garden.

Jenny had turned into so many different people over the years, and Trish had loved them all: the baby with that laugh, the toddler with all those questions, that precocious girl, setting up a tent by herself in the garden and then stubbornly spending a night out in the cold, Trish and Sol joining her, the moon turning green through the plastic. She missed the shy 11-year-old, even the mouthy 14-year-old. She just wanted to talk.

The doorbell rang.

Sol got up. Trish returned to her emails.

'Who was it?'

'Next door,' he said. 'The kids want their balls back.'

She watched him enter the garden. He picked up all the tennis balls and then threw them over the fence, one by one.

2

Kids didn't even say thanks. Soon as the balls were over, they were back at it. Cricket bat making contact. The bone-crack of ball on brick as one of the kids hit a six. Couldn't be much of a match in a garden that small.

Sol thought back to games on the common, West Indies vs India. Old Stevie who'd insist on joining in even though he could barely walk a chain, let alone run one. A real character, they used to say. Always dressed to a tee, Stevie would give Sol shit when he saw him in a basketball jersey. If you were fielding near him, he'd break formation to tell you about the time he trained with the Windies. And he'd come up with odds on the spot – 4/1 Jat goes out with a catch, 7/1 three fours this over. And Jat would get caught out after three fours and Stevie would say, 'You see? If I had money, I'd be a rich man.'

There was a strange logic to the teams those weekends. Jonathan, who was Guyanese, played for the Indians. A few of the Pakistani boys asked to be part of the West Indies. Sol would often ferry between the two to make up numbers. Both teams wanted him to bat for them.

He'd much rather have been playing basketball. There weren't any good songs about cricket, about West London. He felt like he'd been born in the wrong country. He could see himself going to see the Knicks, walking around Brooklyn and Queens, down Linden Boulevard, and all the places he heard in Tribe songs. Every memory of those years had A Tribe Called Quest playing in the background. The bus ride to work, for example, was the exact length of *The Low End Theory,* so that when the 140 pulled into Heathrow, 'Scenario' would be playing on his Walkman, Busta Rhymes going off. He'd take a detour on the way to the control tower, to 'get a coffee', to see Trish. Crush did not do it justice.

She was normally with that guy, Sol couldn't remember his name. Was always making her laugh. To be in with a shot, Sol had to distinguish himself. He tried to become serious, clever. Man, he even started reading the books Old Stevie was always recommending. He worked hard, saved up. Felt himself becoming the man he'd been pretending to be. Got to the point he didn't even mind about Trish, he just wanted to be better.

When she got her job at the firm, he was promoted to Aerodrome Controller. They got married the year *Beats, Rhymes and Life* came out, and Jenny was born a few weeks before *The Love Movement*. She was 18 by the time Tribe's next album was released and Phife died. They both got up first thing the day that Parklife tickets dropped: A Tribe Called Quest were headlining.

He had to get three tickets – Jenny wanted her friend, Priti, to come. Sure, she was a nice enough girl, but the music had always been father/daughter time. They wouldn't even invite Trish. But Sol paid for the tickets without complaining. He deserved to indulge; he'd gone six months without betting a pound.

Jenny and Priti stayed with some friends and Sol went to a Travelodge. They met in the queue the next morning. They went from tent to tent; the girls seemed to know every single act. He was turning into Trish, he joked, feeling out of touch. In the EDM tent, Sol was questioning his decisions when Jenny checked her phone and looked up at him.

Tribe had pulled out of the festival at the last minute. He went to get a drink. This had been Tribe's final tour, and now he was a middle-aged man in a field full of twenty-somethings dancing to music he couldn't even pretend to like. He left early.

He got a taxi to the casino he'd passed that morning. He barely took out anything. He set an alarm on his phone to go off in two hours, 'LEAVE', and warmed up with some Blackjack. At one point he was up a hundred but left the table down fifty. Still, what was fifty in the grand scheme of things? Like, two hours in the control tower? He sat down at a poker table. He got some looks, his shoes still muddy from the festival, his old Tribe shirt worn-out and faded.

He played cautious. Passing time. First few rounds, he folded at the flop or the turn. But then he was dealt the most exquisite pair of Queens and held out to the river for a three of a kind. The sound of chips pushed across felt. Little clacks as he stacked them up. Now he had enough for the petrol home, now enough to take Trish out, enough for the next few months of the mortgage. Hadn't felt this good since that night in Bush, an all-nighter at Paul's where Sol had cleaned up. He'd met Trish and Jenny at Westfield in the morning, and watching them play on the computers, bought them new phones on the spot. He wondered what he might get them now – he had a straight from five through nine and bet heavy. But Mr Cufflinks came out with a full house. Sol played steady a few rounds, until he felt a flush coming. His alarm went off and he apologised.

The sound of his phone brought him back to the present. The kids next door were arguing over an LBW. Sol checked his messages. It was his sponsor, Kaz. He'd been messaging her all morning. Kaz had hit her rock bottom a few years before they met at Group. She'd been planning to move to Spain with her husband for ages. When her son, Gujan, got to sixth form, they even went out there to look at places. They found a place near Vigo and returned home to get things in order before putting down any money. She was worried about spending so much, and not having enough to support Gujan. Or that's what she told herself. She made some big bets.

The circle analysed Kaz's story in a simple way: she was afraid of change and achieving something that had been a dream for so long. She self-sabotaged to maintain the status quo. Sol thought the circle's diagnoses were overly simplistic. His problem, for example, was apparently straightforward. Every day, he worked long hours in the control tower, analysing the runway, giving clearance for take-off. He had to be stable and alert. After work, it was only natural he craved something where he wasn't in control, where he could embrace the thrill of free fall.

'I keep getting those ads,' he texted. 'I don't want the apps but its also like what's to stop me?'

'Classic Sol,' Kaz replied. 'You pre-empt the urges to feel more in control of them.'

He didn't know what to reply. After a few seconds, she sent another message: 'how's the news thing going?'

'Still in 90s.'

Since starting furlough, Sol had been watching a few minutes of archival news footage from every month since the day he was born. Brought back all sorts. Like the other day, Michael Jordan scored forty, beating Philly, taking him up to 15,000 points total. He remembered taking Trish to a sports bar that night, rushing home when the game was over, desperate to be together. Ancient history.

One of the tennis balls landed back in the garden. He remembered the picnics they used to have when they moved in, Jenny's first uncertain steps. Remembered that night they camped out in the green tent. When Trish and Jenny were asleep, he sneaked out and went to Paul's. He arrived in the morning with croissants.

'I went out to get you treats,' he said, unzipping the tent. Could still remember their smiles.

'90s good times,' Kaz replied, with an emoji of someone dancing.

Trish started talking. Another meeting. Her jargon was foreign to him. She sounded so professional. He thought about whether he felt emasculated, her leading meetings while he was furloughed, but decided that was him pre-empting emotions again. What he really felt was curiosity. For years, she'd lived in this other world for eight hours a day. The meeting ended and another began. There was a bit of small talk and then someone mentioned the virus.

'You can almost forget,' Trish said. 'Then it hits you. I've got a friend who works in the funeral business. He says he's busier than he's ever been.'

Sol didn't know of any friends who worked doing funerals. He sat back down in front of the TV that Trish had muted. The historic broadcast was from March 1993. Blizzard in the US. Three hundred killed at the Air India building. North Korea leaves the Nuclear Non-Proliferation Treaty. *Unforgiven* wins Best Picture. April 1993. A plane carrying the Zambian national football team to a qualifier in Senegal crashes, killing all thirty on board. Sol had no recollection of any of it. There was no doubt that he'd read about it when it happened. At what point had his brain decided it wasn't useful information? He could recite almost all the lyrics on Tribe's 1993 album, *Midnight Marauders*, but couldn't remember any of these crashes and explosions and killings.

Another ball landed in the garden. Sol picked them all up and threw them back over the fence.

'Thank you!'

Without missing a beat, the kids were bowling and batting again. He sat on the grass and listened to his wife's meeting through the open backdoor. With Jenny gone, he wasn't quite sure what it was that was keeping Trish with him. At times, love seemed such an intangible reason. Intangible didn't mean insignificant, he thought. It was like the feeling he got when he was at work, looking out at the runway, clearing a flight for take-off, that feeling when that huge thing started to speed down the tarmac and somehow took flight. How something so heavy could fly never stopped looking impossible, but it was a series of intangible things, slight shifts in the flaps, all that invisible air passing through the turbines.

Trish sat down next to him.

'The wifi cut out,' she said. 'I think I'm still frozen back there.'

'Oh, what a shame. You can't work,' he said, drawing her closer. 'What a shame.'

She handed him her mug and he took a sip of her tea.

He heard the meeting resume inside, the wifi returning. Before she could get up to go back, both of their phones rang. Jenny was calling their group chat. Trish quickly answered, all excited, and Sol leant his head against hers so that they could fit in the frame.

Jenny and Trish caught up, and he listened. Jenny wasn't enjoying her new job. She was thinking about quitting, but no one was hiring. She couldn't exactly go back to babysitting.

'It's just as important to know what you don't want,' Trish said. 'If you hadn't gone for this job, you'd never have known and would have always wondered. The only way to be certain is to try.'

They talked for a while longer, and then Jenny left. Trish ignored her meeting. One by one, the balls landed on the grass, the children laughing. Trish turned and rested her head in his lap, and they both looked up, not a cloud in the sky, not a single plane.

Chatpata: Ahankar

AMAN HAD BEEN THINKING ABOUT THE COOKBOOK since Thailand. It was the first time she'd seen Kabir since they'd separated, and they ordered more than they could finish.

'It's all expensed,' he said. 'I'm supposed to taste as much as I can.'

The waiters arrived. Ember-grilled rice with banana-blossom petals served with seasoned crispy bass, Isaan sour curry of snakehead fish and Indian taro stalks, grilled banana leaf packet of blue swimmer crab, Chiang Mai laap of guinea fowl, crisp alliums, somsa citrus, live river prawn wok-tossed in samphire sauce, ceviche of wild amberjack and white turmeric.

Each dish, Kabir explained, was based on a recipe from a nangsu anuson ngansop, a funeral book. People published tributes to the dead, filled with their loved one's favourite stories, prayers and recipes.

She got the call from Dad a few months later during the evening rush. She could hardly hear him over the sound of the kitchen. She imagined him on the ancient landline in the living room, that knot in the cord that no one had been able to undo.

'It was quick,' he said. 'Which is something.'

She finished the dish she'd been plating and left. By the time she reached JFK, she couldn't remember what meal it had been, couldn't remember telling her manager she was leaving, couldn't even remember how much she paid for the flight. She strolled around Duty Free not sure what to do with herself and ended up buying a Senzoku bar gift box. It was a 'European Edition', and she worked her way through each chocolate bar at the gate and then on the plane: Pastel de Nata, Strudel, Clafoutis aux Cerises.

When she landed at Heathrow, in a moment that she would never be able to explain to herself, she stopped at Starbucks to buy a frappuccino. She'd never ordered one before, let alone from a chain. She should have been in a rush, should have at least taken it to the taxi, but she sat in the café area and took her time with it, sip after sip until the white noise at the bottom of the cup.

The front door was open when she arrived. It had been years since she'd seen the house so full. The women sat on the sofas, talking about Mum and the men sat in silence at the dining table. Dad was going around with a tray of tea. Aman found Simran in the kitchen, dal on simmer. Aman couldn't remember what they said to each other, how they comforted one another, but she remembered the bland taste of that dal, the roti with no butter. The simplicity of the meal seemed appropriate, but Aman could only think about what Mum would have said: *we can't serve this to guests.*

For those weeks of avsose, Aman stayed in the kitchen. She needed to keep busy. She made some of Mum's favourites, chole bhature, methi roti, kheer. She noticed that Simran wasn't eating.

Kitchens took on the personalities of their cooks, Aman thought, and she enjoyed living in her mum's shoes for those weeks. She snacked on monkey nuts, remembering how she used to eat them with Mum while watching *Home and Away* together. Simran was allergic. She found a jar of mango achar that Mum must have made a few weeks before she died. Mum's achar was always too spicy for Simran and Dad, it was only the two of them who would eat it. Sharing food was a way of experiencing the same thing, occupying, for the space of a dinner, a similar state of mind as someone else. The communal meal was a bonding moment in most cultures. Maybe that's how her cookbook could start, Aman thought, death as a coming together, food as a bridge. She jotted down notes as she cooked.

She kept the kitchen door open so she could hear the conversations in the other room. She listened to her younger sister tell stories about their mum that Aman had never heard before. Where had she been when Mum was telling them? Simran talked about Mum's childhood friend, Mandeep, who she often mentioned in stories, apparently. Mandeep owned a tandoor in the pindh, and

Mum would take her atta to her to cook. 'She could have made the roti at home,' Simran said, 'the cooking was just a pretence.' They'd gossip about neighbours, 'there was always too much to say in too little time,' Simran said, as if she herself had been there, decades ago in Punjab, 'so Mum said she would take extra atta just so they could talk longer. And then she'd feed the spare roti to the birds.'

On the third day, Aman and Simran went to the crematorium to wash the body. It lay on a raised metal table, a kind of shallow bathtub. The table looked custom built for this very purpose, and Aman imagined it being someone's job to design bathtubs for crematoriums, someone's job to deliver and install them. Was there a specialist company that made them? Or was it a product that conventional bathtub companies offered? She thought of the machines that shaped the metal, the people operating them. She realised, looking at it, that she had no idea how metal was made, or where it came from. Simran prayed and washed the body down. Aman didn't know what to do. She picked up a jug, a plastic thing not unlike the jug they had in their own bathroom at home. She poured water over the body. She didn't know how long they were supposed to stay, how long it took for a body to become pure.

The front door had to be taken off its hinges to fit the coffin in. They set it on the dining table. The rest of the downstairs furniture was taken out into the garden. Upstairs, Aman noticed that Dad's bed had been moved into Mum's room. They covered the floors with white sheets. Relatives started to arrive, queuing single file so that they could walk up to the coffin. Mami Ji burst out crying and Simran took her away, talking about chardi kala. Aman went out into the garden and watched her nieces and nephews play amongst the furniture.

Aman cupped her hands in front of her and the Baba dropped some parshaad into them. She closed her hands, the oil warm, and held them up to her forehead before opening them to eat. It didn't just melt on your tongue but in your palms. It was golden brown even in the Gurdwara's industrial-grade lighting. Now that the service was over, people started to stand up and chat. Aman shut her eyes and took another bite. The parshaad was hot enough that it burned ever so slightly down your throat like a strong spirit. It went down so easily that she imagined her insides as smooth and shiny as her oily palms. Like kids, Aman and Simran went back for more.

The two of them used to hate having to go to the Gurdwara. But they loved getting parshaad at the end. Sometimes, they'd sneak off and play games in the hallway, Simran too young to understand any of Aman's rules. Occasionally, they did seva in the kitchen, the bibiya telling them off. Or they were roped in to Saturday School, sitting through lessons on the five evils: ahankar, krodh, kaam, lobdh, moh. Ego, anger, lust, greed, attachment. When it was time to go, they'd head back to the hall for more food.

Simran took another handful of parshaad. Aman was glad to see her eating. They sat together until the hall emptied. Aman wanted to say something but didn't want to interrupt her sister's thoughts. She wished she could know what she was thinking.

They spread the ashes in the Grand Union canal. A few cyclists passed, a teenage couple hand-in-hand. Aman returned to the spot on her daily walks. It was there that she phoned the restaurant back in Manhattan to hand in her notice. There that she decided to stay and work on the cookbook. She had some agents interested.

When Dad returned to work, Aman decided to surprise him at the restaurant. It had changed management since she last saw it. Now, you entered a small waiting room filled with sepia-toned portraits and newspapers from the turn of the century. A typewriter sat useless on a wicker coffee table. The maitre d' – there was a maitre d' now – stood in a starched shirt, his moustache stiff with wax. He called her Madame.

Inside, ornate fans spun in time to the palatable sitar music. The walls were a rich mahogany, antique hunting rifles were mounted at angles, there was a tiger's head stuffed in an unending growl. The waiters were brown, the bartenders white. The menu came in the form of a newspaper, each plate a headline. Pau bhaji promised a taste of the real Bombay. The coronation samosas came with a side of the Raj's chutney, Nanny's roomali roti with the house dal. While bending towards recent trends – okra fries, turmeric lattes – the menu stayed true to the hits, tikka masala, butter chicken.

She thought then that this might be the closest thing to an authentic Indian restaurant that she had ever been to, in that, sitting here, in her wicker chair, in front of a waiter who had bowed a little when introducing himself, she felt like a white person, rich and royal. To her surprise, most of the customers were South Asian. She expected that the place created this sense of colonial nostalgia for white patrons, that the apneh might find it distasteful. But no, they were having a great time – what the restaurant did was to allow everyone to partake in that twisted nostalgia, it turned the tables so that you, whoever you were, could finally sit at the head.

'The guys thought you were a critic,' her dad said, when she met him in the kitchen. They went out back to have a cup of the royal chai tea.

The previous manager had wanted to shake things up. He said that these days, there were so many Indian restaurants that it no longer mattered if you sold good curry, it mattered that you sold *authentic* curry. They printed new menus and added in spelling mistakes. They created a window into the kitchen to put the cooks on show. At peak times, two of the waiters would dress up and dance to bhangra down the narrow gap between tables, moustache tips as curled as the ends of their shoes. The final aspect of the 'ambience' was the clientele.

'It's not like the old days,' the manager said. 'The goreh actually like to see some apneh when they eat. They take it as a mark of authenticity.'

And so, on a rota basis, for the first few weeks of the grand re-opening of A Passage 2 India, the families of the staff were invited to eat at the restaurant at a high discount. They were told to wear Indian. Aman remembered arguing with Mum about dressing up. When they read the menu, they had to act surprised that the restaurant served dishes as rare and impressive as keema and matar paneer. After that, they were told not to speak too much English.

'Wouldn't even feed this to the birds,' Mum said in Punjabi.

'I like it,' Simran said, in her English accent. 'It's not too spicy.'

'That's the problem,' Aman said. 'Not spicy enough.'

'That's the thing with you, Aman,' her mum said. 'You're always too much. Everything is always not enough.'

Aman learnt more at Dad's restaurant than in Mum's kitchen. Sometimes she'd stop by after school and help to peel ginger and garlic. When she finished, she could shadow the cooks, and they'd eventually explain what they were doing. She learned how to make things like saag and bhindi, would proudly take a tiffin of her food to school the next day. She decided she'd become a chef.

'A cook?'

'A chef.'

'All this education and you want to be a cook?'

'A chef.'

'You think your dad does those horrible shifts in that place so that you can grow up and do the exact same? No, he works hard so you won't have to work so hard. So that you can get an easier job with better pay. And then your children get an even easier job with even better pay. If we didn't make sacrifices like that, we'd still be on the farm. Is that what you want? You want to be the first generation not to move forward?'

'Dad likes his job.'

'You don't know hard work.'

'Then let me find out.'

She started to cook for herself. While the rest of the family ate dal or sabzi, Aman would make new dishes like aglio e olio or ratatouille. Her dad and sister would taste her experiments, but never her mum. Aman wanted her mum to see that the one thing that she prided herself on, her ability to cook, Aman could do better.

When her mum took on extra sewing work in the evenings, it was decided that Aman would cook for everyone. Sometimes, she'd be up late enough into the night trying to perfect madeleines or macarons that she would hear the clothes van pull up at midnight, would see Mum drop off the bin bags of finished dresses and bring in her work for the next week.

The culinary school had a prestigiously small cohort. Her bench was next to Kabir's; he was always by her side, part of her mise en place. If she'd overstuffed her bouquet garni, he'd lift it out of her stock before Chef came. After a particularly humiliating group crit, she stayed behind to show him how to truss his bird. When her sauce was runny and she hadn't noticed, he'd drop some arrowroot into it when she wasn't looking, though he only told her this a few weeks into their second year, when they started to meet up after class.

'Are you telling me I wouldn't have passed if it weren't for you?'

'I'm telling you we're a good team.'

She buttered the paratha, sighing as it hissed. No matter how hard she tried, she just couldn't get them right.

'Mon dieu,' he said, taking a bite. 'I could die. I could actually die.'

They ate like royalty on those weekends, squeezed together in that small, hot kitchen, sleeping through the afternoons – a tradition they tried to keep up when they moved in together after graduation and then relocated to New York. When she got work at a restaurant, Kabir seemed happy enough to keep their tradition alive on his own; she'd arrive home and find him in bed just how she'd left him.

On her lunch breaks she sent out job applications on his behalf. He found out when he got an interview at the Holy Cow test kitchen. He was furious. She was an egotistical control freak who couldn't bring herself to admit that she needed some high-flying partner. If she thought she was so much better than him, if she really thought he was so useless why didn't she just – he went to the interview and got the job.

It was a vegan start-up that was developing frozen burgers. After taking all sorts of tests he was given the title of 'supertaster'. The name went straight to his head, he'd nudge her food around his plate, and say, jokingly, 'A bit rich, could use some lime.' She laughed along, but she was self-conscious about her sense of taste. At the restaurant where she worked, the food was praised for being refined and sophisticated. To Aman, the tastes were so subtle that they barely registered. One time, the sous chef stopped two of Aman's plates at the door. While the waiter was holding them, she called Aman over. 'This and this, the portions are big enough to kill us. You understand? You'll run us to the ground. It's too much.'

Some nights, Kabir would come home with some of his fake meat.

'Look, it bleeds.'

He'd make her blind taste-test his burger and a beef patty. She remembered the days they used the blindfold for sex. She took a bite. The first time she'd eaten beef was at culinary school; she didn't understand what the fuss was about but could clearly tell which burger was the fake.

'They both taste bland,' she said in Punjabi, smiling. And then, in English, 'that's crazy, hun, they taste exactly the same.'

He turned vegan. They started to cook separate meals. The relationship had set in a way that felt permanent. To bend or change now would mean to break. He was happier at his job than she was at hers. He earned more. They hardly saw each other. But one day he arrived at her restaurant and took her out to lunch at her favourite dosa stand.

'I've found this place,' he said. 'If I can get some money from my parents, I think we could afford it. Restaurant-ready kitchen. I've been doing a lot of thinking.'

She phoned home after signing the paperwork.

'An Indian restaurant?'

'No, just a restaurant.'

'Well, what kind of food will it be?'

When Ambrosia opened in Brooklyn, her dad emailed her every review as they came in. Generally, the critics were impressed. She flew her family out to see for themselves. She barely recognised Simran. She did her best not to look at the pagh, or the hair that was growing between her eyebrows. She tried to act like her becoming Amritdhari was perfectly normal. But she wondered if Simran wanted her to react in a big way. She couldn't be sure, couldn't read her the way she used to.

Ambrosia was so busy that she struggled to get them a table. But as the months wore on, the buzz dulled. There were great reviews for a new restaurant every week. Customers moved on. When new ones came, they often seemed disappointed at the lack of normal Indian food. 'If I wanted pasta, I'd have gone to Dinapoli's,' she heard one customer say when she was working front-of-house. 'There's not even tikka masala.'

The vegan options weren't selling so she cut them from the menu. Kabir's rage returned. As numbers continued to drop, she decided they would reposition themselves as an Indian restaurant. With a cringe, she wrote up on the blackboard: 'classics with a twist'. There were countless arguments with Kabir in which he'd drop his bombshell: 'You're turning into your mother.' Even that lost its edge. She found out he'd applied for a job in Japan.

Ambrosia shut. She got work as a cook in a place in Manhattan, the kind of restaurant that only received bookings from people's assistants. Kabir moved to Hokkaido. The company he'd joined was aiming to revolutionise the high-end chocolate bar market. The original Senzoku bar was popular in East Asia, and they had big ambitions for the West. Kabir would be working on special editions; part of thinking global, his cover letter had said, was working local. He travelled the world in search of flavours for his limited-edition chocolate bars: Salmiakki, Buri-Wrapped Suman, Shuku Shuku, Arroz con Leche, Vitumbua, Saffron Halwa, Ras Malai. She read on his blog that he believed every dish had an essence, you could go so far as to say a soul, and while he could never recreate them in a chocolate bar, he could gesture towards them honestly, could hint at that essence.

'Bakwaas,' her dad had said on the phone. 'Not everything needs to be something else. Chocolate can be chocolate. Ras malai can be ras malai.'

They could agree on that. And Aman had repeated that line jokingly when she met up with Kabir on her holiday in Bangkok.

'Let's agree to disagree,' he said.

'We were always good at that.'

'Some of us better than others.'

The snakehead fish arrived. 'So, you've given up the whole vegan thing.'

'You can't be vegan in Japan.'

'We're not in Japan.'

'People change.'

'Maybe in *presentation*,' she said, quoting one of his blog posts. 'But if you boil each element down, the *essence*, that's the same.'

He laughed. 'Glad you've been paying attention.'

They ate, and she let the growing silence become his responsibility to end. He finally thought of something else to say. 'How are your parents?'

'They're good. Mum's a little ill but sounds like she'll be fine. I called them earlier, they're giving out food tomorrow for Vaisakhi.'

'Nice.'

'That's the harvest festival,' she added. 'New year.'

'Isn't it actually about the birth of the Khalsa?' he said, in that way only he could, making a question a statement.

She stopped herself from snapping back. 'They do it every year. It's cute.'

She couldn't manage any dessert and watched him take one bite of every option on the menu, typing notes on his phone.

In the morning she wandered around second-hand stores looking for the funeral books that Kabir had mentioned the night before. She bought any English copies that she could find. Back in New York, she cooked all the recipes included in the books, tasting her way through other families' memories. She wondered what her own nangsu anuson ngansop would include, what she would write if her dad died, or her mum.

By the time she decided to stay in London, the cookbook was writing itself. She wanted to include memories to frame the recipes, and mixed in with each memory were countless others, so that as she wrote, her mum became clearer in her mind. She could see her watching her soaps, phoning in to vote for *Britain's Got Talent* each year, getting angry at the neighbour's constant piano practice. Aman remembered her spending hours cooking saag, patiently sifting through lentils looking for stones, trying, once, to bake a cake, which didn't rise and wasn't served. She was a person who strove for excellence no matter the circumstances and wouldn't settle for anything less than perfection. What had been infuriating to Aman as a child now seemed admirable; her mum would never settle for a lesser life.

This Vaisakhi, she found her dad in the kitchen, already cooking. Aman warmed up last night's parathe and the two of them finished off the last of the mango achar. She made a mental note to add the mango achar to the book. She washed the empty jar, but no matter how hard she scrubbed, the tint of haldi remained on the glass, golden in hue.

She rolled out some dough and dropped the little puris into the oil. It was nice to cook with her dad. He always seemed so calm.

If only she could have as simple and straightforward a life as him: marriage, kids, a decent job. How easy things would be. He was always talking about the simple joys.

It was the third year that she'd gone to the nagar kirtan with Dad. They arrived in Southall and began to hand out the food. A few kids kept returning for more.

When the food was almost out, her sister joined them. The three of them ate. The puris still had a strong crunch, the imli water overwhelming the mouth, cool and bright, followed by the warm earthiness of the potatoes, onions and chickpeas. Sour, spicy, sweet.

Afterimage

FARHAD WAS ON DIVERSION. He turned, the indicator ticking on as he headed down a road too narrow for two cars to pass, let alone a bus. There was a knack to the indicator: if you turned left, you had to signal right to switch it off, but someone was approaching now, and Farhad didn't want to confuse them. The car slowed at a speed bump, its high beams boring into his retinas, so that when he looked away and blinked, two glowing orbs hovered over the street. Rain was falling now but rising on the windscreen. The teenager in the priority seat was fast asleep and he wondered if he'd have to wake her when they arrived, which they would in a matter of minutes, the streets almost empty this late. He remembered the man a few years ago who hadn't woken up, the long wait for the ambulance. Or back in his National Express days, waiting between jobs at a service station, drifting in and out of sleep in the Costa seating area, the coach he was supposed to be driving stuck on a hard shoulder several junctions north, though no one had thought to radio him. The coffee was discounted for drivers so he always got a cup, though he didn't care for the taste and suspected the caffeine fuelled his migraines that would sometimes last for days, floaters obscuring his vision, his mind fried and static, thoughts sinking in waves of white noise, like when those kids hacked the bus intercom, grainy laughter coming through his radio, horrible words, the most horrible things. The car finally passed and Farhad nodded to the driver who he couldn't see. The trapped balls of light in his eyes bounced up and down on the road and he remembered his long walks to school, bouncing his football on the pavement, remembered practising kick-ups alone at break. One day, the boys in his class came up to him when their ball was confiscated and invited him to join their game. Though he wasn't allowed out of goal, he played well, well enough that they tolerated his taking part, he made the teams even, after all. He'd been a Manchester United fan all his life, wore his Beckham shirt proudly on mufti, which made the others laugh, Beckham having moved on to another team long ago, the shirt a cheap fake. On his 18th birthday, his mother bought him tickets to see United play a friendly at Wembley. They played their reserves, but that was okay, from their seats you could barely make out the names on the backs of their shirts. Farhad had cheered, rising for the Mexican Wave. He had thought then that this might just be the centre of all happiness in the world, the beautiful game, he called it, in all seriousness, listening to the matches every weekend on his mother's radio. Even when he got his own TV, he listened to the games, preferring the sounds of the commentary and the gravelly cheers to seeing the match for real. When he listened, it was as if he could experience the game in first and third person, being at once in the stands and in each position on the pitch. His daughter called him an old man for listening rather than watching and he sometimes wondered if this was one of the details by which she would one day remember him, a quirk that became a defining feature. She'd enjoyed football as a child but had long gone off it. One summer he'd volunteered to coach her team, did she remember? He'd loved it, willing the kids on, teaching them the importance of formation, of flow, but it hadn't lasted long, apparently some of the kids had complained that the way he spoke was too hard to follow and a group of parents took him aside and said it was time for him to go. How do you explain that to your eight-year-old? They'd taken the bus home from practice, and she'd fallen asleep next to him. Behind them, a couple talked in another language. Whatever they were saying seemed very important, they sounded so passionate, and he couldn't decide then, heading down the Ruislip Road, whether they were happy or angry. A young man across the aisle was drawing; he'd look up at the woman standing at the doors and then look back down at his page as he sketched. The woman got off at the next stop and Farhad imagined the teenager's unfinished drawing, the outline done but the face without features. He pulled up at the penultimate stop now, and someone got on, which was strange, the bus's destination only a matter of metres. The passenger tapped her Oyster and half-looked at Farhad with a slight smile. Someone paying for such a short journey had a story, he thought, they all did. He imagined how she saw him, a blank man behind the screen – on any given day, he was seen by hundreds of people, but how many would remember his face? How many even registered it? She headed up to the top deck, and he felt ashamed, it was likely she'd got on the wrong bus, or in the wrong direction, and didn't know. The other drivers made fun of his tendency to feel sorry for his passengers – if he ever saw someone running for his bus, he would wait. This one time a middle-aged man ran a block to reach him. When he got on, he couldn't find his card, and started to cry. Farhad let him through and checked on him on the monitors every few stops: he wept and wept. He'd have liked to have comforted him, but terrible things happened if you ever left the driver's seat before your destination. Other drivers said there was an actual curse, which was nicer, Farhad thought, than thinking that the public were just horrible. Once, Farhad had stepped out to stop a fight between two schoolboys who looked like they might actually kill each other, and he got placed on leave for touching a minor. He remembered the weeks at home feeling as if time had slowed, he thought about going out and doing something, making the most of it, but he stayed in, listening to the incessant steady ticking sound that went on throughout the day, one of the machines in the flat playing up. He couldn't find the source and when he described it to his daughter, she said it was a scenario straight out of a comedy show: there's always an episode about a sound in an apartment driving someone crazy, she said, it normally turns out to be the batteries in the fire alarm, or the Carbon Monoxide detector. He didn't have a clue what she was on about and they spent that afternoon, or evening, watching the same formulaic episode play out in *Friends*, *The Big Bang Theory* and *It's Always Sunny*. She had so many theories, but Farhad couldn't concentrate, looking at a screen that long gave him a headache, listening to that studio laughter made him sad. The ticking turned out to be the extractor fan in the bathroom, which he replaced himself. Seeing his reflection, screwdriver in hand, he saw his father, what little he could remember of him. His father had a scar on the back of his head, and Farhad would often ask where it came from. It was always a different answer, or at least that's how he remembered it: an accident, a birth defect, a fight. Farhad would sit behind his father on car journeys and would run through each of the stories behind the scar, which was the shape of Japan. They were driving to Bisotun, Persepolis vs Esteghlal on the radio, the car having to stop at different points for his mother to throw up. Seeing her double over with motion sickness dispelled the image he often had of her as someone faultless, or at least that's how he thought of it now, how her throwing up made her a person in her own right, a person with problems of her own, not just his mother. That day they had finally parked in the shade of the mountain, and his mother stayed in the car, too tired and ill now to go for the walk. So Farhad and his father followed the trail around the mountain from one carving to the next. His father told him about King Darius and King Khosrow. His father let him wear his aviators – he remembered the cool shade they threw over everything, how they were too big for him and would slip down his nose, the natural light seeming so bright as to look unreal. They stopped for a long time at his father's favourite inscription. There were three languages, he said. Truly ancient, he said. Can you believe something could survive so many thousands of years? Farhad hadn't been able to properly see the inscription, but he googled it years later when Bisotun was announced as a World Heritage Site. Apparently, the main cause of damage to the monument was that Allied forces used it for target practice in World War Two. He turned back onto the usual route now, heading towards the final stop at Haven Green. He remembered, as he often did when he reached this final stop, sitting with his daughter and watching a few kids kickabout on the other end of the green. Their ball had come rolling over to him, one of the boys walking after it. With a short run up, Farhad laced the ball the length of the field back to them. It was the perfect kick, the cleanest kind of connection. He sat down, certain of himself, and watched the kids pass the ball between them, left and right. The indicator ticked. The woman on the top deck came down. The teenager in the priority seat woke up. Farhad pulled up and let them off. He indicated right and then turned off the engine. He watched the two of them leave, walking together until the teenager turned towards the station and the woman continued on. He shut his eyes for a moment, imagining the lives they were going on to, the people they would see, slight traces of light still pulsing on his eyelids, still there.

The Piano

———

AFTER HE'D DONE THE EVENS, Paddy did the odds. For the five years that it had been on his route, the road was like any other, neat rows of newly planted trees casting speckled shadows over semi-detached homes. But doing his rounds a few weeks ago, Paddy saw a group of old men dragging a piano out from fifty-eight and onto the pavement. And from then on, it was the road with the piano.

At first, Paddy thought it was for the taking. He could see it in his dining room, his little one learning to play. But one of its legs was bike-locked in place. There was a stool tucked under it. Wasn't a sign or anything. It was simply there.

Passing it each day, Paddy would run his finger along the keys, high to low. He hadn't seen anyone play it until now. He posted a letter for fifty-five and looked across the road. A young man sat down on the stool.

*

Umer rested his fingers on the keys, playing silent notes, waiting for the 90 to go. In the month since he started working, he'd walked one way to the chicken shop. But today, he'd left a little earlier than he needed to and, on a whim, gone a different way. He wondered how long the piano had been here, only minutes from his home, without him knowing. He tentatively voiced a chord.

He tried to improvise a little something, but repeating the move-ment, he realised it was a song he knew, nothing new under the sun and that. He switched up, jumping into a stride with a Fats Waller pomp, before stumbling onto a minor refrain that he came at side-ways, thinking Thelonius Monk. Over the static of growing traffic, he looped a Dillalude, gliding into a familiar Soulquarian groove. Melodies came and went like passing thoughts, and cars, with their windows down to let out smoke, slowed to hear him hum Badu over The Twelfth of Never.

*

Priyanka's bus pulled up. Hearing music, she looked out the window. A man was playing a piano on the street. He was wearing a red cap and matching polo shirt. She took a photo and sent it to her group chat. The replies were instant.

'He's kind of fit you know'

'TF is he wearing?'

'Have we finally found priya's type?'

'Thought this day would never come'

Priyanka replied with a Forever Alone meme.

'All that time playing pain gonna final come in useful'

The girls used to crowd the practice room at break when she was preparing for her piano exam. She'd run through her pieces, and they'd chat away. She'd taken up the piano to strengthen her university applications. It was supposed to indicate she was a person beyond her studies. But then the music became its own type of academic pursuit. The bus moved on, and Priyanka glanced back at the house behind the piano, all its windows open.

*

Reggie stood in the family room listening to the music. The piano was Vi's. He'd given most of her things away, but the piano had remained, silent for months.

She'd been standing right here, by the window, when it started. She coughed. 'Must be something going around,' she said.

They went to the GP. They went to the hospital. Lung cancer.

A few weeks later, he went for a check-up of his own. The doctor found a benign lump and suggested watchful waiting, whatever that meant. He'd left Vi at home to rest. When he reached the doorstep, he could hear her playing her piece upstairs. He put the key in the door but didn't turn it, listening.

Vi was determined to keep living life. She filled the calendar with all sorts. Janelle, their daughter, came with them to appointments, closing her hair salon in the middle of the day. Reggie rolled the strange words around in his head: cisplatin, etoposide. They sat next to Vi during chemo, watching, waiting. At home, he cooked and cleaned. There were still bins to take out, grass to cut. There was respite in scrubbing tiles, relief scouring mould from grout.

After chemo, Vi flushed her system clean with water. They were both in and out of the bathroom all day. That was the extent of his own little mass, an endless feeling of needing to go, and the frustration of never arriving. He went to check-ups almost hoping for the thing to malign. It would be neat, he thought, that after a full life together, they would die together. He couldn't imagine life without her, and there was something romantic in the thought of dying in each other's arms. Or at least in neighbouring beds.

When Reggie was finally admitted – a routine procedure, the doctor said – Vi was an inpatient. Janelle taught them how to talk to each other through computers. The connection in the hospital was off and on. When the call buffered, Reggie hung up and redialled. They picked up where they left off, going through old stories, playing the hits. After years of marriage, they knew them all by heart. But they were like old songs, the kind that when they came on you couldn't not sing along. Vi did the one where her foot got trod on by Nina Simone. Reggie that one about the salmon.

The connection cut. Vi froze, lit blue by her screen. Reggie redialled.

'Where was I? Right, so I climbed through the window–'

'Some might say fell.'

They were young again, talking all night, the first signs of the sunrise filling their separate rooms.

'Sing the sun awake,' he said.

'It's late,' Vi said. She always did this dance.

'It would make my day. Do the one you wrote.'

She sang under her breath. People were sleeping. Her voice was fragile but perfectly clear, like thin ice. There was a delay in the connection, and he watched her mouth move a second or so before any sound came out, like she was miles away. She froze.

He made his recovery in time for the funeral.

The piano player finished and walked off. The day passed as it usually did, both slow and quick. When clouds appeared, Reggie went out with two rainbow-striped umbrellas and attached them to the piano. The rain cleared and the sun returned, casting multi-coloured shadows across the keys. He brought the umbrellas in. He was woken by music in the middle of the night.

*

Mo still knew the intro to 'Still D.R.E'.

'If you ain't up on thangs,' he sang.

Gujan fucked with him, pressing random keys.

'Wallahi, man. Shut up,' Abdinasir said. The bus was late. Mo finally stopped and, taking out his keys, started to carve into the wood.

His trademark 'OM' could be found all over school, passed down in textbooks, etched into exam hall desks and sprayed on the bike shed. Other students had taken to adding extra letters to the tag: omg / coma / blossom / vomit / omen / Amy will you go prom with me?

'Seriously.'

'It's an artistic statement,' Mo said, mid-O. 'It represents spirituality.'

The bus arrived before he could begin the M.

*

Amrit was not impressed. She'd come into Jagmeet's room just to complain. 'It's not so much to ask, peace and quiet,' she said.

'Can we just go back to sleep?'

'That's the point. I can't sleep. Three nights in a row now.'

'They've stopped.'

'It's not right. It's not good for my blood pressure.'

'It's teenagers being teenagers.'

'It's two in the morning. Can't you ever agree with me? Does there always have to be something?'

Jagmeet rolled over.

*

Amrit went next door in the morning. Reggie was already outside, putting the umbrellas out.

'I'm sorry but this can't go on,' she said. 'All this noise.'

'Is this about last night? I'm sorry. I could put up a sign.'

'I'm not sure why it's here in the first place. It's blocking the way.'

'My wife died,' he said. 'I wanted it put to good use.'

'We can agree that last night isn't good use.'

'Well–'

'I think it's best we take it in, no?'

She walked off, followed by the postman, who ran his fingers along the keys.

*

The postman gave Reggie a letter. It was for Vi. Reggie wondered how long she'd continue to receive mail. How many databases was she on? He took it up to the spare room and sat at the desk. There were still rings in the wood from her cups of tea. Still indents of the piano feet in the carpet.

He put the letter in the drawer and picked up the pile of sheet music Vi had left out on her last visit home. He couldn't read music, but he often looked over the piece, tracing the shapes of the notes with his finger, as if it were written in braille. He tried to remember the tune.

He crossed off today on the calendar. It was personalised, his last

Christmas present to Vi. He flicked back to January. It was filled with her colour-coded notes: social green, work blue, doctor gold. He turned to February: Judy's 90th, Janelle down. March: Reg's bday, check-up 3pm, piano tuner. April: hosp 11, bank, hosp 4.30. The rest was empty, apart from Reggie's crosses.

Above every month was a photo. Reggie's favourite was August. Vi dressed up for Notting Hill 84, smoking, not long after they first met.

Reggie was staying on his uncle Mont's sofa when he first heard her. The walls were so thin he could hear not just the notes she played but little thuds of the pedals, odd creaks of the woodwork. Mont complained about it, but when the neighbour played, Reggie tuned him out.

When he left to move into his own place, he paused on the way out. He knocked on the neighbour's door. Whenever he told people how they met, Reggie would say: 'Now, I was expecting anyone. Could've been a man. Could've been a pensioner. I was knocked off my damn feet when Vi opens that door.'

'Course I took *him* out,' Vi would say, when asked about their first date. 'Otherwise, we'd have ended up at his local.' They saw an old Brazilian film at the BFI and walked along the Southbank afterwards, going in and out of bars, their words misting up ahead of them.

'Sleep's for the dead,' they said, missing the last train. They walked around the quiet city, talking, and in the empty carriage of the first morning tube, she sang the sun awake like the character in the film.

They met at carnival rehearsals. Vi was in a choir, and Reggie was in over his head drumming. He'd never been to Notting Hill before, never touched an instrument – 'but if it meant seeing Vi,' he'd say, 'I'd have done a drum solo wearing nothing but sequins and feathers.'

The procession itself was a blur. All he knew for sure was that he ended up with Vi, sitting between two overflowing bins, sharing a

Red Stripe, planning a future together. It wasn't long until he and a team of friends were struggling to move her piano into their new place. They sat in the back of Mont's van and Vi played while they were stuck in traffic. He'd never forget Uncle Mont's face when they arrived at the house, and she asked if they could put the piano in the spare room upstairs. She'd practise in the evenings, and Reggie would listen through the bedroom wall.

He heard music outside and opened the windows.

*

Priyanka opened the book at random. She'd found the music up in the attic with the rest of her schoolbooks, neat handwritten notes between the staves, 'use left hand', 'key change'. Hearing Ms Li's voice in her head, she straightened her back. Ms Li had at least one ring on every finger and when she played, they'd click. Some of the other students called her Knuckle Duster, and one claimed to have seen her on the weekend, with multiple toe rings. Looking at the sheet music, she could remember the steady encouragement in her teacher's voice, the metallic sound of her clapping out the time.

Her fingers felt awkward at first, but slowly the feeling came back. She topped the bossa rhythm with a little melody, and from the medley of notes two phrases emerged, circling one another like dancers in a crowd. The wind blew the pages to another song, but she carried on, pulling out of the chord progression to two lines repeating and repeating, two singers left behind by the procession, not yet done celebrating.

A girl on a scooter stopped to listen.

*

Ayan liked the piano lady. She listened a bit before scootering off super-fast. She stopped, looking left right left right. No cars. Then she scootered super-fast down the straight bit where she didn't need to push. Stop. Look.

'Someone's singing, Lord. Kumbaya.'

Mum had had it up to here of her practising for assembly. Home was for inside voices. Green man, wake up. She scootered kind-of-fast up the up bit, near where Dad lived.

'Someone's crying, Lord.'

When she reached Dad's road, she turned back. This was as far as Mum let her go.

'Kumbaya! Kumbayakumbaya!'

Now the up was down and the down was up. 'Someone's praying, Lord.'

At the corner, near the piano lady, there was a man leaning against the fence, nodding his head, tapping his toes. Ayan scootered past super-fast.

*

Umer didn't want her to see him. It was the first time he'd heard anyone else use the piano. What were the odds that someone from round here was as into music as him? And what were the odds that she looked like that? She switched key and sped up. When she finished her song, he turned down a path in his life he'd never have taken before: he walked up to her. She was flicking through her sheet music.

'Hey,' he said. 'I heard you. You're good. Great.'

'Yeah?' she said, looking up as if she recognised him. 'You play?'

She stood up and he took a seat. He played his take on 'If the Moon Turns Green', and standing next to him, she added a melody. He hit the odd bum note, nervous – he was rushing, he was sure of it.

*

She pretended not to notice. Priyanka couldn't help but think, as she harmonised, that this could be a story she might tell one day. This weekend to the girls, maybe in a month to her mum – who knew, who knew?

It started to rain, but instead of getting the bus, she decided to walk with him, and they began to talk.

*

Reggie came out with his umbrellas. He was determined not to have a speck on the woodwork. He'd already had to fill in some circle scratched into the side, had to clear up the crumpled cans of Tyskie someone left near every night and bin the laughing gas canisters that some kids had taken to throwing at the keys. These little tasks helped fill his days, days that were more or less the same. He didn't leave the house in case anything happened to the piano.

Janelle came down to stay often. He liked spending time with her but found it hard to talk. They discussed the rude neighbour, who Janelle had talked down. They watched TV together; she introduced him to box sets. The episodes went on and on. Sometimes, looking at her next to him, he felt increasingly certain that if she was forced to choose, she'd have had it the other way around. He could imagine her and Vi doing things together after he passed, going to concerts and restaurants, determined to keep going. Vi would have been better at grief than he was. She would have been a better parent. He imagined Vi organising Janelle's future wedding, imagined her as the ideal grandparent. She would have looked after the little one when Janelle was at work.

He carried on with the box sets after Janelle left. When his favourite piano players arrived outside, he'd pause the TV and listen. He wanted to be at that wedding, to play with that kid. Wanted to be more like his wife. Go somewhere, do something. He looked out through the net curtains.

*

Umer arrived first, just as it started to spit. He'd been meeting Priyanka at the piano before his shifts, taking his red work clothes in a
bag. This was the third day in a row, was that too keen? He thought
he should dial it in. He checked his hair in the window of a parked
car and sat at the piano. He was wearing a chain that he'd ordered
online. He couldn't tell if she'd like it or not, and after sitting at the
piano a minute, he took it off and put it in his pocket. A pigeon
landed on the pavement, flying off as a girl passed on a scooter. Priyanka was normally here now by now. Maybe she wasn't coming.
She probably wasn't coming.

*

Priyanka got off the 90. There was Umer. It was beginning to rain.
The consensus on the group chat was that it was time to meet
somewhere other than the piano. That way she would know if this
was just about music, or if it was something more. She checked
her breath and then approached. She ran her finger across the
back of his shoulder, and he turned and smiled, making room on
the small stool.

*

Reggie found the piano players sitting together. He fumbled with
the umbrellas and stopped to catch his breath before talking to
them. 'I love how you two play.'
    'It's really nice of you to let us use it,' Umer said.
    'I haven't been able to practise since school,' Priyanka said.
    'Well, that was the dream. Couldn't bear for the thing to go to
waste,' Reggie said. 'You know, my wife wrote this,' he said, handing
them a colour photocopy of her piece. 'This was her piano; I was
wondering if maybe you might give it a try?'
    He walked slowly back into the house.

*

Priyanka took the lower half and the Umer the higher. They started slow, the high notes responding to the low, the lull between chords filled with the sound of rain on the umbrellas. There were sections where only Priyanka would play, and Umer would follow the notes on the paper, scared to look down at her hands, across at her face. And then Umer would start, his touch gentle, maybe too quiet for the piece. For the most part, their sections were separate, but as the pages turned, their hands got closer together. Umer, all staccato, picked out a quickening melody as Priyanka rumbled frantically from chord to chord to keep up. For a moment, their feet met at the pedal. The beat fell in tempo. They worked their way back up, and following Vi's colour-coded writing, ended with a crescendo. Their separate motifs fell into line and, a few octaves apart, they played the same notes.

'From the top?' she asked, though he'd already begun. She looked up from the page and watched the net curtains dancing through the window, wide open despite the rain.

Haven Green

———

Though we're not so self-
important as to think everything

has led to this, everything has led to this.
Nicole Sealey, 'Object Permanence'

THE TWINS KNEW SOMETHING WAS UP. They were playing their cutest selves, old enough now to keep themselves entertained. Usually, Jyoti wouldn't let Jenny out of her sight. After dinner, Jenny put a film on for them and they didn't argue about what to watch. Jeevan fell asleep on her lap. Jenny should have taken him up to bed but didn't. And when Aman, their mother, came home from her restaurant to let Jenny off, the boy was still there, his hands in small fists.

The calm didn't last long. The next time she was over, they refused to go to sleep.

'I want Priti to read the bedtime story,' Jeevan said. 'She does it better.'

'When's Priti coming?' Jyoti asked.

'She's not coming,' Jenny said.

'Next week?'

'She won't be coming anymore. It's just me now.'

They preferred how Priti made sandwiches. Why couldn't Jenny just bring her over like normal?

'It's grown-up stuff,' Jenny said.

'Grown-ups are boring,' Jeevan said.

'You're not wrong.'

'Is she coming next time?'

They wanted the songs Priti used to sing. Jenny googled the lyrics.

'What is greener than the grass? And what is smoother than the

143

glass? What is louder than the horn? And what is sharper than the thorn? What is deeper than the sea? And what is longer than the way?'

She paused like Priti used to and they shouted their answers.

'Water's smoother than the glass.'

'A fart is louder than a horn.'

Then she continued. 'Envy's greener than the grass, flattery's smoother than the glass, rumour's louder than the horn, slander's sharper than the thorn, regret is deeper than the sea, but love is longer than the way.'

Jenny took the twins for a walk through Ealing. She avoided the high street – as far as she knew, Priti still worked at the café – and they headed towards the park. She peered into the large windows of the double-fronted houses. She remembered looking out at them as the E9 entered Ealing, Priti by her side, because Priti was always by her side, the two of them picking their favourites.

When Jenny first got the job babysitting for Aman, she phoned Priti on the bus home. 'You wouldn't believe the house. Parquet floors. A claw-foot tub.'

'French doors?'

'French doors.'

'Oh God. Stop.'

They used to watch reruns of *Grand Designs* at Priti's after school and make plans for their ideal place.

'Are you going to get divorced?' Jyoti asked, as they arrived in the park.

'We weren't married, silly.'

'Yes, you were,' Jeevan said.

And the kids talked about the afternoon when they'd married Jenny and Priti, napkins for veils.

Jenny sat on her favourite bench. There was a faded plaque set into the weathered wood: *In loving memory of Montgomery and Jeanine Richards.*

'By that logic, you two are married, too,' she said. The twins had got jealous that day and had a ceremony of their own.

'Gross.'

'We already got a divorce. I signed a prenut.'

'You what?'

'Girls have to protect their money, that's what you said.'

'You remember everything, don't you?'

'I can remember when I was born.'

'Really?'

'Yeah, I sneezed, and mummy cried.'

A few weeks after Jenny started, Aman agreed that she could bring Priti over to help. 'But I'm not paying both of you,' Aman said. 'It's a one-person job. It's on you if you bring a friend. And I don't want anything happening under my roof, you hear? This is more than most would allow.'

They were freer in Aman's big house than they were at their own. Here they could be the people they wanted to grow up to be.

'I know it's awful,' Jenny's mum had said, when Jenny told her about the break-up. 'But it's good it's happening. It's an important part of growing up. If you stay together forever, you'll always wonder what could have been, all those other closed doors. This is just part of life. One day, you'll look back and this will all seem so small.'

Everyone she told echoed those lines. Young love was supposed to end. It was a phase everyone went through. Older people seemed to believe there was some threshold you crossed in your late twenties, where real life began, and that everything before then was a kind of game, make-believe. They seemed to suggest that the feelings you had as a young adult or as a child were at best lesser versions of what you would one day feel. But when the twins were sad or happy, Jenny had never seen anyone as sad or as happy. If anything, she thought, our most intense feelings happened when we were youngest.

When the twins were awake, Jenny wished for peace, but when they were down the quietness was unbearable. She tried to distract herself with Netflix, but a new season of hers and Priti's favourite show had come out and that was enough to make her cry. She remembered the one time she watched an episode of it without Priti.

'You've betrayed me. I feel betrayed.'

'It was a moment of weakness. It meant nothing to me. I'm so sorry.'

'I just – I need space.'

'If it helps, I thought of you the whole time.'

They laughed. 'Our first argument,' Priti said. 'We can tick that off.'

Jyoti appeared. Jenny wasn't sure how long she'd been looking at the Netflix home screen.

'What's up?' Jenny said, taking her into her arms. 'Can't sleep?'

'I woke up and thought everyone was gone,' she said.

Jenny sang a lullaby that occasionally worked during Jyoti's colic phase.

'I gave my love a cherry that had no stone. I gave my love a chicken that had no bones. I told my love a story that had no end. I gave my love a baby that's no crying.'

She was already forgetting what Jyoti used to look like, what she used to be like. She could only recall the same few scenes of her early childhood, and the more she replayed them, the clearer they became and the further any other memories of her drifted away.

'How can there be a cherry that has no stone? How can there be a chicken that has no bones? How can there be a story that has no end? How can there be a baby with no crying?'

Jyoti shut her eyes. Would she remember her, when she was Jenny's age?

'A cherry when it's blooming, it has no stone. A chicken when it's pipping, it has no bones. The story of our love, it has no end. A baby when she's sleeping, there's no crying.'

The weekend before her birthday, the kids baked Jenny a cake.

'Wow, what flavour is it?'

'Red.'

'Red?'

'With sprinkles.'

She let them watch YouTube on her phone. From the kitchen, she heard them giggling and talking. She could have sworn she heard Priti's voice. She found them on FaceTime to her. Jyoti was standing on the windowsill showing Priti a plane that she'd spotted outside.

'Did they call you?' Jenny said. 'Or did you–'

'These geniuses phoned me.'

'Sorry. You can go if you want.'

'What? No, I miss you guys. What have you been up to, Jyoti?'

'It's Jenny's birthday party. You're invited!'

Jenny watched them talk, and then Priti asked the kids to put her on. She took the phone back to the kitchen.

'How are you doing?'

'You know.'

'Yeah. I really miss those kids.'

'You're all they talk about.'

'Are you okay?'

'Can we do cameras off?'

'You're boring now,' Jeevan said. 'Why won't you play with me?'

'I am playing with you.'

'You're not even holding your gun.'

Jenny picked it back up.

Jeevan repeated his instructions. 'You're Russia and I'm America and when I shoot you, you have to die like this.' He fell to the floor, gasping for air.

He shot her and she died.

'What happens if I shoot you?' she said.

'That's not the rules.'

'Then why do I need a gun?'

Priti used to have such patience for his games. And she managed to get them to do proper activities, baking, arts and crafts, gardening. No, Jenny thought. That wasn't true. It was Jenny who'd got them planting seeds in the garden. She knew she had a tendency to turn her every weakness into one of Priti's strengths. If only knowing about a problem fixed it. It was tiring to be more aware. She was so tired, she realised, lying dead on the floor. She was exhausted. But her sadness had such stamina.

'Get up! Rewind!'

Jenny lived a full bus route away from the twins. The stop closest to Aman's house, Haven Green, was where she used to meet Priti. She would visit her at the café even before they were official. They fell in love waiting for buses, people-watching from the backseats, one earphone each. Jenny would walk Priti home from her stop. They'd slow their pace as they approached her house and as soon as they parted, Priti would phone her, not wanting her to walk alone. And though they'd just seen each other, they had so much to talk about, there was just so much to say.

The kids wanted aloo parathe. Priti used to make them, thin and crispy. They tasted just like the buss up shut roti that Jenny's grandpa used to make. Jenny took a copy of *Chatpata*, Aman's cookbook, from one of the bookshelves, and found a paratha recipe. Her dough was too wet and then too dry and none of her attempts were round. When she served the kids, she expected another 'Priti did it better ...' comment, but they said nothing. Maybe, she thought, they'd finally begun to move on. She wasn't sure if that was better or worse than the idea that they still missed her.

By the time the bougainvillea bloomed, the kids had forgotten the day they'd planted it. The bright pink petals held their attention for a brief moment before they continued with the water fight. Jenny was in charge of refills, which made her neutral, but they fired at her anyway. She retaliated with the hose. They laughed. But then Jeevan made Jyoti cry and Jenny had to separate them.

'Why don't you get a new girlfriend?'
    'I don't know, Jyoti. It's not that simple.'
    'I have two boyfriends.'
    'You do?'
    'Yeah, it's easy. You just hold hands.'
    'I'll bear that in mind.'
    Jeevan joined them. 'Did you know there's seven billion people in the world?'
    'That's so many people, isn't it? And how crazy that out of all the billions of people, the three of us could meet? Do you know how many millions and millions of things had to happen in the exact way they did for us all to end up together?'
    'And did you know there's ten quadrillion ants in the world?'
    'Quadrillion isn't a word,' Jyoti said.

The twins wouldn't sleep. Jeevan wouldn't brush his teeth and Jyoti was hiding somewhere. How much easier it was when she and Priti could take one child each. The memories of those nights had collapsed into one idyllic image, the kids tucked in and Priti singing. 'I'll love you 'til the bluebells forget to bloom. I'll love you 'til the clover has lost its perfume. And I'll love you 'til the poets run out of rhyme. Until–'

The next Saturday, Jenny took the kids out for McDonald's. They passed Haven Green. It was time to move somewhere else, Jenny thought, to a place that held no memories. What she really wanted, she realised, was to be able to be someone else, even for a moment, to get out of her head. How cruel it was to be thrown into this big world, and to only see it from one small angle.
    The kids fought over their Happy Meal toys. Jenny took Jeevan

to the toilet, leaving Jyoti to finish her nuggets. But when they returned to the table, she was gone.

The place was packed. She picked Jeevan up and rushed around the restaurant. She couldn't see Jyoti anywhere. She asked the servers, but they hadn't seen anything. She took Jeevan into the men's and women's toilets, calling out for Jyoti. All the stalls were empty. The cashiers had checked the CCTV. She'd walked out alone. Blue raincoat, blue shoes.

Jeevan was crying now, asking to be put down. Jenny had never seen Ealing Broadway so busy. There were so many people – all potential threats. So many shops, so many roads coming off the high street, and so many roads coming off those. Cars sped by. Jyoti was a quick runner. She could have been anywhere. Jenny rushed in and out of shops, looked down alleys. Was she in the shopping centre, at the park, heading home? Jenny tried and failed to think like her.

She arrived at Aman's restaurant. She could hardly get the words out. Aman called the police and ran out. Jenny gave Jeevan to one of the line cooks and left with the waitresses to cover more ground. Everywhere she looked, she saw glimpses of blue. She ran around the park, calling her name. She took out her phone to check in with Aman and saw three missed calls from Priti. She phoned her back.

'Jyoti's here. Where are you? She's come to the café. I called Aman, but she says they were with you.'

Jenny ran to the café.

'They just left,' Priti said, hugging her. Her hair was back to its natural colour. She smelled the same. 'She was fine. She wanted to show me her Happy Meal toy. I made her a hot chocolate.'

'Was Aman–'

'I think she was just glad Jyoti was okay. She didn't say anything.'

'I just.'

'Come on. Sit down.'

Priti went to make her a drink and Jenny's breathing slowly steadied. Jyoti's toy had been forgotten on the table by the window. Jenny put it in her pocket and took a seat. The people around her continued to eat and drink. Acoustic covers of pop songs played on the radio. The coffee machine groaned and hissed; cutlery clinked on ceramic. Priti finally joined her, setting down two coffees. She asked about the kids, about what had happened before Jyoti disappeared, what it was like to look for her. Jenny answered, watching people pass outside. More customers arrived, but Priti didn't get up to serve them. She sat with Jenny until they finished their drinks, the two of them quiet now, despite having so much, too much, to say.

Be More Roy

WHEN MONT ARRIVED AT GREENFIELD, Miriam had been there a year. The bell rang and his sister Judy left. He was taken to the dining hall, which, as his buddy Roy explained, everyone called the Mess.

'It's always a bit of a mess.'

You were given a buddy when you joined. Mont didn't like that, made him feel like a kid. As did the red plastic tray, the angel cake for pudding. He sat down next to Roy, said hello to the others. He didn't pay much attention to the men around the table. Way he saw it, wasn't much point getting attached.

That first dinner, Miriam came up to their table.

'Mont?' she said, catching him off guard. She must have heard him introduce himself.

Next time he saw Miriam, Nurse Aanshi was walking her around the garden, wearing those rubber shoes Jeanine liked to wear around the house.

'Remember when you used to wear Jimmy Choos?' he'd laughed, when he'd first seen them.

'Yeah, I need these *because* of those Jimmy Choos.'

Miriam and Aanshi walked up and down the lawn like swimmers doing laps. It was the kind of still summer day where kicked-up dirt hung in the air. Bees went door to door in the flowerbed, the beheaded stems of stubborn weeds emerging again. Mont sat on a bench by the small allotment plot and watched the vapour trails of landing planes slowly fade, pink in the late-afternoon light. A bird, maybe a robin, bounced about the bushes. Roy's strawberries were starting to show. Mont tried to focus on his feet on the ground, the feeling of the bench on his legs, the way Jeanine would tell him when they used to go and sit on their bench in Walpole Park. *Feel your fingertips, your palms, the breeze through your hair – what's left of it.*

Aanshi dropped Miriam off next to him.

'Do you mind?' Miriam said.

'My pleasure.'

The two of them sat in silence, the robin here, then there.

'Did you live local?' she said.

'Only down the road. I actually remember when they built this place. We used to laugh at the name. My wife said it's where they put you out to pasture.'

'I grew up around here, too. Then we moved out to the country-side. When I left home, I went straight back to the city. And now, all I can think is how nice it would be to be back in nature.'

'That's the way the world goes round.'

'It's not much of a place,' she said.

He wasn't sure if she meant the city or the home. 'No, not really,' he said.

'Could you walk me to my room?' she said.

It was the strongest he'd felt in a while, her hand gripping his arm. Her room was full of pictures. 'They don't let you stick any-thing up,' she said. 'But my son got me this Magic Tape. It comes right off. You can take some if you'd like.'

Mont nodded, looking at a photo of a painting of the sea.

'You got kids, Mont?'

He shook his head.

'I've got just the one,' she said, propped up on a pile of pillows.

He turned to leave.

'You really don't remember, do you?'

Judy came with her son, Reggie, and his wife, Vi. They looked through old photos. Judy named every single person.

'So how are things here?' she said.

'Good, good,' Mont said. He knew she was paying a lot. 'All good.'

'People treating you nice?'

Mont smiled. 'You'll like this. There's a woman here who says that she was my girlfriend when we were kids.'

Miriam and Mont sat together at Roy's service. They were told not to be sad, that he would have wanted this to be a celebration.

'Everyone always said Dad was good people,' Paddy, his son, said. 'He taught me a lot. How to be a better man. "We could all be more Roy", people used to say.'

Mont took Miriam for a walk after. As Roy had been his buddy, he was expected to go to the circle talk. But that didn't feel right – he barely knew him. It was only his third week.

'We got chips after school,' Miriam said. 'Remember, there was that chippy on Lady Margaret?'

He remembered a chippy.

'We got chips and you asked me to be your girlfriend. Just like that.'

'Did you say yes?'

'Not straight away – who do you think I am?'

'What? I wasn't good enough?'

'You clearly were. I couldn't think straight for a week. Everyone fancied you.'

'Well, *that* rings a bell.'

'I said yes in Ravenor Park, walking to school one day. We were so happy.'

Mont's new buddy was Balwant. It was Mont's job to show him round. When the bell rang, he went to Roy's old room. Balwant's family was still there, his son talking to Aanshi.

'It's really not acceptable. We're paying a considerable amount here. It's not too much to want walls without marks all over them.'

'I know sir, I agree, I do. The room was thoroughly cleaned. We have a policy.'

Mont peered inside. There were a few Blu Tack marks on the walls. He didn't know if he should go. The son was saying something else, but Aanshi told him visitor hours were now over. It was dinnertime: routine was key.

'This is the dinner hall,' Mont said, leading the way. 'People here call it the Mess.'

Balwant wasn't much of a talker. Mont introduced him to everyone sitting down at the tables. He couldn't spot Miriam.

'I told you,' Miriam said, when he saw her again three days later. 'It was a planned procedure. I did tell you.'

'Well, how do you feel?'

'Like someone's cut me up and sewn me together again.'

The bird was back, one branch to the next.

They strolled down their usual conversational paths, until they were back to her favourite topic. 'You know how they told me? Not even over dinner, no kind of lead up to it. Just passing in the hallway one day, my mum goes, "We're moving at the end of the year." It made me so angry. I was so angry.'

'I'll bet.'

Two planes looked like they were headed for a collision. They passed by each other in the sky. Mont wondered how far apart they really were.

'Imagine how things might have turned out if I didn't have to move.' The bird jumped to the grass. 'Can you imagine?'

When visitor hours were over and Judy had gone, Mont would pop by Miriam's. Her son lived far away. He always had work.

'He used to tell me off when he was a boy,' she said. 'A lot of the time, I was late to pick him up from school. Now here I am, sitting around all day, waiting on him.'

'That's the way the world goes round,' Mont said.

She was gone for a week this time. Didn't feel planned.

Aanshi wasn't sure when she'd be back. 'You two seem close. Is there something I should know?' She smiled.

'Funny story. Miriam says that we actually knew each other when we were kids.'

'Does she now? It's amazing what that one will remember.'

When Miriam returned, Mont had to wheel her out on their walks. Up to the end of the garden, round to the bench. He parked her next to it and they shared the armrest.

'You took me to the cinema. That was so romantic. No boy had ever taken me to a movie before.'

'What did we see?'

'Oh look, she's got a worm.'

The bird pecked at the ground.

'My son called,' she said, after a pause. 'He says he's coming down.'

'That's great.'

'He'd only come if things were serious.'

Miriam's son shook Mont's hand and turned right back to the nurse.

'How's she been?'

Mont didn't understand why he couldn't just ask Miriam that, when she was sitting right there. Judy did the same thing when she visited. No one trusted them to be able to say how things really were. Mont left them to it. He put the TV on in his room. John Wayne. Miriam wheeled in halfway through the film. 'He had a call,' she said. 'He's on call.'

He caught her up on the plot and they watched it together. At the showdown, he looked over at her. She was fast asleep. Like a light.

It was Battenberg day at dinner. Bal didn't touch his piece and Mont gave it to Miriam on their next walk.

'You remembered!'

Battenberg was her favourite. She split the slice into squares and gave him the pink ones – she liked yellow. He closed his eyes as he ate, something he'd always done with desserts, something Jeanine would laugh about. *What are you, praying?* When he opened his eyes, Miriam looked a little off.

'All good?' he asked.

'He says the home he's got me into had a waitlist of almost two years. That it's where he wanted me to go in the first place.'

It took Mont a moment. 'I don't get it. You like it here.'

'I do.'

'So, I don't get it.'

'He's the one paying.'

'But it's your life.'

'Mont.'

'He's your kid, you're the one in charge.'

'Mont.'

They phoned each other after breakfast, before they each went for their walks.

'Is it fancy?'

'It's very fancy,' she said. 'It's so green. They have grounds, Mont, *grounds*. There's a pool. What are we going to do with a pool?'

Mont laughed. 'I can barely handle the shower.'

'How's everything there?' she asked.

'Good, good,' Mont said. 'Same old.'

'This won't work if you're like that, Mont. You've got to talk. What did you do yesterday?' Mont wrapped the cord around his finger, making a ring. 'Or today?' she said.

It was hard to call every day. Sometimes Mont slept in, and there were lots of activities at Miriam's new place, cookery, book club, something called Pilates. But that didn't mean he didn't think of her each day. When he woke up, the first thing he'd see was the painting she'd given him, the one of the sea, magic-taped to the wall by the window. Then he'd go for his walk, watch movies, play cards with Bal. That man wouldn't talk for days, but if you got him a deck of cards, he wouldn't stop. He loved to explain the rules of different games, would talk you through your first round, drumming his fingers on the table, laughing like hell when you lost. Sometimes Bal's granddaughter, Raveena, would come, and she'd always kick up a fuss, running around the Mess. Sometimes they played snap, and once they did a picture together and Mont showed her how to draw birds in the sky, little open books. He tried to focus hard on all the details so that he could talk about them to Miriam later.

'Hey Bal, you remember Miriam?'

'Miriam?'

'She used to live here.'

'Oh,' Bal said. 'Sorry.' He put his hand down.

'No, no, nothing like that. You'll like this though. We met here right, but we actually first met years and years ago, when we were kids. We used to be boyfriend and girlfriend. I can remember it all so clearly now, Bal. We used to walk home together after school. We used to go to the park all the time. You ever been to Ravenor? Not far from here. Had our first kiss in that park. I took her out to the movies once, saw an old Western. I got us milkshakes. Man, I've always loved milkshakes. Even now. An old man craving a strawberry milkshake.'

Miriam called him that night. She was watching a live broadcast on TV. Apparently, there was a chance that a Near-Earth Object could collide with the planet tonight.

'There's twenty thousand asteroids within collision distance of Earth,' she said.

He turned on his set and watched along. 'Is that so?'

'Twenty thousand. Makes you think.'

He thought about it. 'Sure does.'

The cameras were showing a starry sky. He imagined the asteroid arriving in a blaze, leaving a smoking crater where London had been.

'They say it could cause an extinction event.'

'Bal's little granddaughter came by today,' he said. 'We had milkshakes.'

'Doesn't even have to be that big, you know, to cause a real catastrophe. A couple miles is all it takes.'

They both looked at the same shot of the sky on their different screens, waiting for the end of the world. But that night, like every night they'd known, it was a near miss. Mont fell asleep, the receiver in his hand, and woke facing the window, with a view of the sea.

Chatpata: Moh

—

'MATA KHIVI WAS THE ONLY ONE of the Gurus' wives to be mentioned by name in the Sikh texts,' the guide said.

The tour stopped in the shade. Simran was out of water.

'She's described as a good person, an affectionate mother, one who provides shelter and protection. In my opinion, she's the most influential woman in Sikhism.'

The white walls of the Akal Takht were too bright to look at, as was the water that people were bathing in, and the golden walls of Harmandir Sahib. Everything was reflecting light. Simran shut her eyes; she'd never heard of Mata Khivi.

The guide continued. Khivi was the wife of Guru Angad Dev Ji. They married when she was thirteen and had four children. After twenty years of marriage, her husband became a Guru.

'You can imagine,' the guide said, 'that overnight, they suddenly had a lot of visitors! She made sure every guest ate well. Guru Nanak Dev Ji is credited with introducing the concept of langar, of free communal food – he saw it while travelling in Persia. But Mata Khivi,' the guide said, 'she is the person who made langar the institution that it is today. She worked to make sure that langar was for everyone.'

The guide described the sixteenth century as an era of extreme wealth inequality and caste prejudice.

'In those times,' the guide said, 'it was bad luck for anyone of a low caste to even see a Brahmin eating. But in Khivi Ji's Langar Halls, everybody – rich, poor, man, woman, old, young – sat on the same floor and ate the same food. And they still do.' She gestured around them. 'One of the slogans of Sikhism, "degh tegh fateh", sums this up. *Long live the pot and the sword.* The pots will stay forever warm because of Mata Khivi. You have to see it as radical. With the introduction of free food and shelter, the very idea of extreme poverty was in a sense eradicated. No matter who you are, what situation you are in, you can eat langar.' The guide dropped to a whisper:

'We aren't supposed to boast. But here at Harmandir Sahib, we can serve up to 100,000 meals a day. All 100,000 of those meals, and all the millions more around the world, they can be traced back to Mata Khivi. Every single one free. That to me is revolutionary.'

A few members of the tour strayed off to take photos. One woman used a map of Amritsar to fan her child's face.

'One of my favourite stories,' the guide continued, with boundless enthusiasm, 'is that Emperor Akbar once visited Guru Amar Das Ji. Normally, when courting someone of such stature, you would prepare the most elaborate private banquet.' Simran had heard this story before. When the Emperor arrived, he was made to take off his shoes and enter the Gurdwara. Before they talked, they ate, and the Emperor had to sit on the same floor as everyone else, putting him on the same level as the Guru, the priests, the soldiers, the cooks. The Emperor was so moved to see all these people of different castes and religions eating together, that he gifted the Guru with a large amount of land.

'Guru Ji humbly refused,' the guide said. 'So, the Emperor gifted the land to the Guru's daughter as a wedding gift. That, ladies and gentlemen, is the very land on which you are standing now. It became the city of Amritsar, *the pool of nectar*.'

Some members of the tour smiled. One yawned.

'Okay,' the guide said, 'without further to do, lunch!'

At the hotel, Simran googled Mata Khivi. She found the quote from the Granth: 'Khivi, the Guru's wife, is a noble woman, who gives soothing, leafy shade to all. She distributed the bounty of the Guru's Langar; the kheer is like sweet ambrosia.'

Simran repeated the line, trying to memorise it. Watching the ceiling fan spin counter-clockwise, she thought of the kheer that she and Aman loved as children, and remembered following her older sister into the Gurdwara kitchen. They could escape the boredom of the main hall under the pretence of seva. While the sevadars were busy making roti, Simran and Aman would sneak over to the giant pot of kheer, the rice pudding bubbling and thick. Aman would fill two bowls and they'd go out the back door and sit in the Gurdwara car park. Now she thought of it, there was no reason at all why they couldn't have just asked for the kheer. In all likelihood, the bibiya knew exactly what they were doing, and didn't care. But she could have sworn the kheer tasted better in secret than it did in the Langar Hall. Simran would blow on hers until it cooled. Aman ate hers hot. The sight of the skin that grew on top of the kheer always made Simran feel a little sick; she had no idea how Aman could eat it. Whenever they had guests over and Mum made tea, Aman would scoop the skin from everyone's cups to eat. The thought of it made Simran want to retch. Now, each time she made Indian tea, those moments would come back to her. She'd remember Mum letting her break open the cardamom pods, would think of her in Dad's restaurant, taking a sip of the 'chai tea' they served:

'Tastes like dishwater.'

'Yeah, I don't want any more,' Simran said, siding with her mum.

'I'll have yours,' Aman said.

'No,' Mum said. 'That's your cup, Simran, you finish it. You need to be more like Aman. Be more.'

After she'd returned home from Amritsar, she flew to America with her parents to see Aman's restaurant. Simran and her dad were pulled out of line by the guards. They walked through the detectors, no sound, no light, but they were told to wait. They were scanned with handheld detectors. Again, no sound. Simran's guard put her hand on her pagh and started to feel around.

They got a taxi straight to Aman's restaurant. There was a queue outside, or at least Simran thought it was a queue – it was hard to tell, people were leaning against the storefront, sipping beers that glowed amber in the warm light that the restaurant's naked bulbs cast. 'Ambrosia' was written in a casual scrawl on the sign, and inside the menu was up on a blackboard, impossible to read wherever you sat. Simran and her parents waited for their table at the door, standing out with their luggage. Despite the delay at the airport, their table wasn't ready. Not that they had a table; after a ten-minute wait, they were taken to the end of a bench next to a party celebrating an engagement.

Simran went to the bathroom. It was a new restaurant, but the bathroom walls had years' worth of graffiti. Simran wondered if they'd had people in specifically to deface the walls, if they'd paid them. She remembered when she went shopping with Aman as a teenager, and how, as soon as they got home, Aman took her brand-new Converses and dragged them through the mud in the garden. She didn't notice Simran watching as she threw the shoes at the ground, jumped on them, scraped them along the patio tiles.

The mirror was covered in stickers. Simran tried to fix what Border Control had done to her pagh. A man walked in and, smiling at her in the mirror as he washed his hands, said 'Namaste'.

Out in the restaurant, Aman was sitting in Simran's seat.

'Simba!'

'Amb!'

It was so good to see her. They hugged and Simran felt twelve again. They shared the space between their parents. 'I've ordered for you,' Aman said.

It looked like Aman would eat with them, but one of the waiters came to get her. Aman's partner had left, and now she had to cover for him; she was pissed, she whispered, her breath warm in Simran's ear, 'He does this all the fucking time.' She paused. 'You still swear right?'

Course after course arrived. Simran had no idea what it was she was eating, though Aman assured her that her dishes were meatless and eggless. The food was different to anything Simran had ever eaten before; within the strange shapes and textures there were hints of familiar tastes, little gestures home.

'I'm blown away,' Dad said, when Aman returned to sit with them.

'It's good,' Mum said. 'Nice.'

Someone asked to have their photo taken with Aman. Then the conversation turned to Simran.

'She's unemployed,' Mum said.

'She's doing all sorts of work at the Gurdwara,' Dad said. 'It's very important.'

Simran didn't know what was worse, her dad's attempts to bring her and Aman together, to make sure they were treated as equals, or the way Mum so easily split them into their separate categories. It was just like when they were kids. Her dad treated her Cs and Ds the same way he did Aman's As. Her mum told her that school just wasn't for her, and that was okay, there was more than one way to cook a potato. It made more sense that she helped her mum with the sewing work than spending all that time revising for exams she was destined to fail. While Aman studied or cooked, Simran and her mum would sew and talk. Sometimes Mum told stories, would talk about her old friend, Mandeep, and other times, as they threaded their needles through the fabric, the two of them would simply sing along to the kirtan on Sunrise: 'Waheguru, Waheguru, Waheguru.'

'You know your Nani Ji,' her mum said, 'she hardly ate. But all day, whatever it was she was doing, she'd do her simran. "Waheguru, Waheguru," like that, all day. That's why I chose your name. And if I ever asked her why she wouldn't eat, she'd say: "amritu bhojanu namu hari." And that's how I got my name.'

Simran had found that line written in Aman's notebook only days after Mum's death. There was a crude translation underneath it: 'God's name is delicious food.'

'What's this?' Simran said.

'Just something I'm working on,' Aman said.

'It's about Mum?'

'Yeah.'

'She wouldn't want that.'

'How do you know?'

'She didn't like all that stuff. The fancy food, the articles.'

'What's up, Simba?'

'Can you not right now?'

'You've been off with me since I got here.'

'Oh, you mean two days ago?'

'I don't even – what?'

'She was ill for months, Aman. Years really. They said the attack was likely. Where were you?'

'I'm sorry I can't just up and leave as easily as you can. I had work.'

'This should all be about her. But this,' Simran said, holding up the notebook, 'is another way to make it about you. Mum's life wasn't about you. It's not yours to use.'

The next day, they washed the body. Simran didn't know what to say, so she repeated Waheguru to herself, over and over, losing herself in the word as she had when she was a child, the repetition almost dizzying so that you couldn't tell where the word ended and where it began. Waheguru, Waheguru, the body washed, the body burned. Waheguru, the ashes gone, the still water of the canal. Waheguru, Waheguru, rolling out atta at the Gurdwara, roti after roti on the pile, the other sevadars gossiping about so-and-so's grandchild who'd married a gorah, or been divorced, or had a child. Waheguru, the Gurdwara kitchen busy with a wedding or a funeral or a baby born, Waheguru, burnt finger on the tava, Mum a week dead, Mum a week left. Visiting Mum after seva, bringing her parshaad in a little plastic bag, the stories she told, how she softened towards the end, sweetness coming through, fruit going off.

'When I was a child,' she'd say, taking the parshaad, 'there was no time of year like the harvest. Following the nagar kirtan through the pindh, all that song, all that food. We were so happy.'

She told Simran that she'd met Jagmeet not long after the harvest. 'He was a city boy. He'd moved to the pindh with his family after the riots. Mandeep knew all sorts of gossip about him. Apparently, he'd fought off a gang that had broken into his house. A brave, strong man, that's what I wanted.'

Mum would often lose the thread of the conversation and pick up in the middle of another story. 'I still remember, when I was pregnant, Mandeep said, "Having children is like working for the harvest. You work and work like a dog all year, but no matter what you do, you can't control the rain, can't control if birds come or if the well runs dry. Even if you could, you'd still have no idea what your crop will be like."'

Simran wished she'd heard those kinds of stories when she was younger. Dad never talked about anything from back then. It was like he'd never even been to India. She wondered why her mum opened up to her so much more in old age. Maybe, she thought, she'd finally proven herself worthy. She cared for her while Aman was off in America. It felt like she was finally enough.

'Needs more loon masala,' her mum said, the last time Simran brought her sabzi to eat. 'And the roti needs butter.'

'You shouldn't be having butter.'

'It doesn't matter.'

'It does. My rule.'

'Your rule? I didn't realise I had to follow your rules.'

'Well, I've spent twenty-five years following yours,' Simran said.

'And all Aman did was break them,' Mum said, as dramatic as a character in one of her soaps. 'And look where she is now,' she said. 'And look where you are.'

At first, she thought that her mum was saying that Simran was a model daughter, unlike Aman who was on the other side of the world and hadn't visited. But then the meaning reversed. Simran had followed the rules, Aman had broken them. But the game had still worked in her sister's favour – Aman was the success.

She was still thinking about what her mum had said months after her death, when she walked to Southall with Aman to sort out the gold. Mum had left them an equal amount and they had to claim it. At the bank, they were taken to a room in the back. Drawers lined the walls, as they had in the crematorium. They were given the box of Mum's gold and a scale.

'Let's just take a piece each.'

Simran took some earrings. Aman took a necklace.

'It's a shame she never got to see us wear any of this,' Simran said.

'Two unmarried daughters,' Aman said, with a fake sigh. 'The ultimate punishment.'

'Don't.'

Simran took some bangles. Aman took a ring.

'You and that Baba at the Gurdwara looked pretty close,' Aman said, handing over the ring. 'Maybe you should have this.'

'Very funny. He's not a Baba, he's not even thirty.'

'Is that a yes?'

'Don't. He's nice,' Simran said. Aman smiled. 'He's a *nice* man. There.'

'Nice men are hard to find.'

'I'm sure you can say that with some authority.'

'What's his name?'

His name was Gurmukh. He sang kirtan at her Gurdwara. His voice would come through the Langar Hall speakers while she cooked, and some nights she'd find a kind of peace in that, her hands and eyes busy with the cooking, her ears and mind busy with his music. Simple joys. She knew he preferred sabzi to dal, would always take three roti. Sometimes, she'd kid herself into thinking he knew her favourite shabads to sing.

She wished she could see him outside of the Gurdwara. And then she did. They recognised each other in a crowded Trafalgar Square, standing in the shade of Lord Havelock's statue, both holding matching placards: *Never Forget 84*.

Simran had been going to the annual march for years, and it felt like the campaign was finally gaining traction. They were calling for the events of 1984 to be officially recognised as a genocide instead of a riot. Gurmukh was just as passionate about it as she was. He mentioned his plans to start an oral history project about 84, he wanted to interview survivors and witnesses.

Eating langar together a few days later, they set out their plan. Gurmukh put a call out for volunteers each time he sang on stage, and Simran travelled around London, and then to Gravesend, Birmingham and Wolverhampton with flyers. After a few weeks, people started to reach out. They recorded the interviews in Gurmukh's kitchen.

They were saying that the Sikhs had poisoned the water. They were saying not to drink the water.

They came in the morning throwing stones. We were told to stay inside. Then they broke in and the fires started.

They tied us up. They were making us watch as they forced themselves on my mother. My father and brother they were screaming. I was too scared to make a noise. One man was holding me on his lap. He slapped me if I was looking away from the bed. It was my bed.

They took us out to the street. They stripped my father naked and my neighbour. They tied their hair together and then filled my father's mouth with kerosene. He was gagging. Then the man put his cigarette in my father's mouth.

I was lucky.

They looted the Gurdwara by my house. My cousin said he saw them urinating.

I was at the station when the train pulled in. I can still remember the smell. They'd gone through, carriage by carriage.

173

No one hurt us. But my father, he fell ill at the time. He was an old man. They wouldn't let us in the hospital. They weren't serving us.

We'd killed the mother of India, they said. Blood for blood.

Wouldn't give us back our clothes.

They arrived at the school. They burned the school desks. Looted the supplies, destroyed the library.

If the Police weren't joining in, they would watch. 'The nights are ours, the days are yours,' they said.

We used bricks, swords.

I read a book on it. It said they used the voting records and school registers to find the Sikh houses. It was methodical and planned. A riot is an accident. But these people they had lists and went through them, ticking each house off.

They took the eyes first.

They had a special technique. I now know it was called necklacing. They'd fill a bike tyre with fuel. Then they'd take a man and put the tyre around his neck. Then they would set it on fire.

I'm sorry.

They said if you want to be freed, kill two Sikhs.

They took everything we had. I was only a small child. All my brothers they turned to drugs. They gave it out cheap. My brothers stopped eating. The opium was how to forget.

When a big tree falls, the earth is bound to shake.

They didn't have to pay for the kerosene. It was free.

They asked if I could identify.

They smashed the bus windows with iron rods and then pulled a Singh out. They tied a noose around his neck and dragged him through the streets. Different mobs took turns.

There was one mob that was castrating. They didn't want us to have children.

Can I have some water?

There's nothing that can be done. All I care is nothing happens more.

Chardi Kala.

Simran would end each session emptied. She'd offer the witnesses food but most refused. It seemed to her that nothing could be more important than this. She felt a sense of guilt when she had to return to her daily life after the recordings. How could she do chores, have a cup of tea, watch TV, and also know that these things had happened? Surely there was more that she and Gurmukh could do? Then she'd feel guilty for fixating on atrocities of the past when awful things were happening every day, right now. But if they didn't, who would? They couldn't let it all disappear. She asked her dad if he could contribute a testimony to the project, but he refused.

Five years after Mum died, and two years after Simran married Gurmukh, an advance copy of Aman's cookbook arrived at Simran's door. It was titled *Chatpata*. Simran had been dreading its publication ever since she read Aman's notebook. She expected it to be filled with warped stories of their mum, stories that would be centred around Aman. But she was pleasantly surprised. It was a beautiful object, clothbound, with an illustration of a mango on the front. Inside, the dedication said, simply, 'for Mum'. And that was the last mention of her in the whole book. There were no anecdotes, no memories or family photos. Just lists of ingredients and instructions of what to do with them.

She took a photo of her dad holding the book for the first time. His daree had gone white so quickly. Aman had cooked a meal, but before they started to eat, their dad began to speak.

'I never saw any use in digging up the past. But I've been talking with a few friends, and I realise it's not good for me to always be keeping things.'

'Is everything okay?' Aman asked.

'You've probably heard from people in the family about the riots. I'm sure your mother told you. You know, my family went to Mata Ji's farm and when my father returned for me, he found me without my hair, injured. I didn't speak for a while. They filled in the gaps.' Simran looked down at her plate of untouched food. Her dad's voice wavered. 'From so far away, it's easy to see the story as the truth. But it never happened how they told it. If I was at the house when they came, I'd be dead. My friend saved my life.' He paused again. 'We were in love. Me and him. Friend isn't the right word.' Aman placed a hand on his forearm. 'I thought it could all be in the past. I was married. I had children. I didn't think anyone ever needed to know.'

'God, Dad, it's okay,' Aman said. She continued talking, saying how happy she was that he'd told them, how much they loved him.

Simran felt her silence change meaning beyond her control with each second that passed. Finally, she spoke. 'Did Mum know?'

Her dad looked at her. 'I never said anything. Maybe she thought it. I don't know.'

'Okay.'

'It was different then.'

'Yes,' Simran said.

Simran and Gurmukh arrived early at Aman's book launch. She watched the bookshop fill up, impressed with the number of people coming to celebrate her sister. Dad arrived with a group of friends. She recognised one or two of them from the Gurdwara. A few of them had been at her wedding. Aman gave a long speech that Simran zoned in and out of, and then she answered some questions about the book. Afterwards, they all headed to a bar. Simran thought it was best that she show her face.

Gurmukh bought her an elaborate mocktail. Her dad and his friends were getting increasingly loud, their table filled with different-shaped cocktail glasses. Small plates based on Aman's recipes were served. Emphasis on small, Simran thought. Her dad was smiling and laughing. And so was Aman. Gurmukh bought her another mocktail.

'I thought we said one,' Simran said.

'We haven't even talked to anyone,' he said.

He took her over to meet her dad's friends. They each had some story to tell. She found herself laughing, asking questions. They made space for her and soon, she realised, she was having a good time. The bar filled up with other parties, celebrating other things.

They worked up an appetite. Some of Aman's friends wanted to go dancing, but she said that she wanted to come with Simran and their dad, who'd suggested getting something to eat. Everywhere was closed. They hadn't realised how late it was. Time had become this slippery thing somewhere in the night: they were leaving the bar, then they were in a giant Uber and then they were at a 24-hour cash and carry, grabbing ingredients, ending up in Dad's kitchen.

It was chaos. They cooked with a kind of mania, too many people in the small kitchen. Aman and Simran stood side-by-side at the hob while the others snacked on nuts and crisps, dipping broken breadsticks in what was left of the hummus. Aman and

Simran made gol gappe and served them with a hodgepodge chaat, followed by some samoseh that had been in the freezer for months. The kitchen filled with smoke as Aman charred the aubergines for bhurtha – why on earth had she decided on making bhurtha at two in the morning? – and they all welcomed the fresh air once the windows were opened. Dad managed to cut his finger while making a redundant salad. There was a comic amount of blood, and everyone laughed. Karan, one of Dad's friends, took over, trying to impress Aman the famous cookbook author with his julienne and chiffonade. Simran was in charge of roti and rice. Aman put together a slapdash sabzi with the rest of the vegetables they'd picked up. Karan asked her what she was going to write next, and she said that she'd been thinking of opening a new restaurant, giving Ambrosia another go but in London. She'd found a space in Ealing. Karan said that they'd all be regulars, they needed somewhere better than Jagmeet's restaurant to meet. Dad raised his middle finger at Karan, who laughed at the pink plaster. Simran couldn't see Gurmukh anywhere. But then he reappeared, a box of fresh gulab jamun cradled in his arms. He wouldn't reveal where he'd got it at this time at night, 'a magician never tells'.

While the others ate the sweets, Simran returned to the kitchen to clean up. She spotted a half-broken puri on the counter and added some leftover filling. She poured in the last of the imli water, and it rushed through a crack and onto her hand. She ate the gol gappa in one bite and then licked her fingers, looking around to see if there was any more.

Freehold

—

WHEN FATIMA SAW HER CHILDHOOD HOME for sale, she booked a viewing. She mentioned it in passing to Yusuf, seeing him at the students' union. They were meeting alone more often now; she wasn't sure what they were. He said it would be fun to see where she grew up, and to hang out again before he flew home for the summer. She thought about inviting the rest of their friend group but didn't.

The estate agent was late. They stood in the front garden, and Fatima peered through the open window of the neighbour's house, trying to see if the same couple still lived there.

'There used to be grass,' Fatima said, kicking at the gravel. 'Dad was big on nature.'

'That's where you get it from,' Yusuf said.

They'd first met a few weeks after freshers, having signed up for the same green action group – well, a friend had signed her up; Fatima had failed to decide on a single society to join. The group travelled around London with bags of wildflower seeds and planted them illegally. Yarrow, cowslip, heal-all. She and Yusuf had been partnered. After spring, Yusuf asked her if she might like to retrace their route and see what had grown. Most of the plants, if they had taken root, had been cut down or pulled out. But there were a few that survived. She took a photo of some of their cornflowers growing by an old fountain. While they talked, a man took off his shoes, rolled up his trousers and stepped into the fountain, filling an old coffee cup with wishing coins.

'Is it how you remembered?' Yusuf asked.

'Pretty much,' she said. A teenage boy was staring at her from the bus stop across the road. She looked away.

They sat on the front garden wall. Yusuf took out his phone. He always typed with one thumb.

'This is my house,' he said, Google Street View open. In front of the house stood a ghostly figure, whose face had been blurred. Yusuf pressed the arrows, taking her around the neighbourhood. 'This was my school. This is where we played soccer.'

Finally, a car parked up. The estate agent came out, followed by a man and a woman.

'Eleven o'clock,' the estate agent said, seeing Fatima and Yusuf. 'God, I'm so sorry. We've double booked. Crossed wires. I can only apologise.'

The two couples looked at each other. The man was Yusuf's height. The woman was pregnant.

'That's okay,' the woman said. 'You can go first.'

'Yes, you go,' the man said.

'I don't mind,' Fatima said.

'We could go together?' Yusuf said.

The five of them squeezed into the hallway. There was new laminate flooring. The wallpaper was gone, but the stairs were the same. The banisters hadn't changed. Now there was a mirror by the door. Inscribed on the wooden frame were the words 'live every moment'. Fatima was careful not to catch Yusuf's eye, or they'd start laughing. They needed to look like serious buyers. She looked at the other couple in the reflection. They were holding hands. She was tempted to reach out to Yusuf.

The estate agent led them into the kitchen that had been extended when Fatima was a child. The rent increased when the work was finished, and she and her parents moved out soon after, looking to downsize.

'It's actually great you're both here at once,' the estate agent said, still flustered. 'Because this house is perfect for people at different stages. You've got great schools, a lovely park a stone's throw. And then there's the transport links, great for commuting, nights out, what have you.'

The fridge was silver, not white, and covered with magnets:

'home is where the wine is', 'keep calm and carry on and on and on'. The handles on the cupboards had been replaced; there was a dishwasher now. Here was the windowsill where Dad's herbs had grown. There, the wall that Mum had thrown spaghetti at after seeing it on TV. Fatima sat in the spot where she used to eat.

The man asked questions. And then Yusuf. He was doing the British accent that always made Fatima laugh. It was disconcertingly accurate. The last time he did it, their friend group had gone Westfield to window shop in the designer stores. He'd had them cracking up in Louis Vuitton and the guard asked them to leave.

'My least favourite genre of people,' Yusuf had said, 'are people with fake authority. Like they get a badge or a uniform and have to act out some power play.'

He was often saying things like that. He had a stance on everything. Fatima, on the other hand, wasn't sure she could state any single opinion with certainty. Things were always shifting.

The estate agent left them to explore. The other couple went upstairs, Fatima and Yusuf out to the garden. The lawn had been paved over. The child-sized handprints in one section of concrete were filled with the morning's rain. Yusuf found a football and they passed it back and forth. She told him about the summer the extension was built. Paul, the builder in charge, had to bring along his daughter, Maja, because of childcare issues. She only really spoke Polish. Fatima taught her words and games. Maja was the younger sister Fatima had long wanted. She tried to convince her mum to let Maja stay the night. She could have used the empty bottom bunk.

When the garden was dug up to lay the foundations, Fatima's dad suggested the girls go look for buried treasure. The builders were off for lunch. He carried them down into the pit and they found six gold coins. Fatima knew the coins were from her birthday, but she pretended they were real for Maja.

'We'll grow a chocolate tree,' she said, burying the golden wrappers in the mud after they'd eaten them all.

'Chocolate,' Maja said to herself. 'Chocolate.'

Her mum wouldn't let them inside because they were muddy. She whisper-shouted at her dad and made them stand on newspaper. Fatima read the words between her feet out loud, trying to impress Maja. 'Crash, bang, wallop. £50 billion wiped off shares. Mega-bank Lehmann Brothers folds.'

When the work finished, Maja left. She didn't live nearby, and they never saw each other again.

A window opened upstairs. They could hear the couple talking.

'I can see us happy here.'

'I think there might be damp.'

Back inside, Yusuf asked the estate agent about transport links, resuming his British accent. Fatima went upstairs. The man was in the bathroom. The woman was in Fatima's old bedroom.

'What do you think?' Fatima asked her.

'It's nice,' the woman said. She was looking at a fish tank which stood where Fatima's bunk bed used to be. 'I think we'd be interested. Are you interested?'

'I'm not sure what we want. That's why we're looking. To get an idea.'

'I remember those days,' the woman said, tapping the glass. 'You'll get there soon enough.'

There was a model sunken city in the fish tank. Colourful fish darted aimlessly around the ruins. Different action figures stood half-buried in the sand like ancient statues.

'They've evolved for millions of years,' the woman said. 'And here they are.'

The fish swam round and round. Through the open window Fatima heard the backdoor open, the estate agent taking a call.

'It's my weekend,' he said. 'It's legally my weekend. She's coming here.'

He walked around the garden.

'It's like you're planning these sleepovers intentionally. There's no way there's this many birthdays.'

He kicked the football.

'Can you put her on? I want to hear it from her.'

Out front, Yusuf and the man inspected the pipes. An alarm was going off next door. Fatima didn't know what you were supposed to do when you heard someone's alarm. Calling the emergency services seemed extreme. But there could be a fire. A break-in. She gave the woman and the estate agent a look to convey her uncertainty. They carried on talking about catchment areas.

It could have been anything. A gust of wind through an open window slamming a door. And it wasn't like she was the only person on the street. If anyone should have done something, it should have been the people that actually lived here.

Then a leg appeared out of the neighbour's open window, followed by the rest of a body – it was the teenager she'd seen earlier. He was wearing a backpack and two handbags and had a small TV under one arm.

'Yusuf,' Fatima called, without thinking.

The teenager saw them and ran.

Yusuf chased after him, and then the man. Fatima followed them, the estate agent and the woman behind. The teenager dropped the TV and the screen cracked. He turned off the road and down the alley that led to the park. The grass was wet, the field empty. The climbing frame was still there, but one of the swings was missing. The teenager ran across the dirt path that connected the two exits. It was the way Fatima used to go to school. The path was muddy, and she was scared of slipping. She almost always wore platforms around Yusuf, not wanting him to see her real height. He was striding ahead now and caught up with the teenager. He grabbed the straps of one of the handbags and then the man, who had also caught up, tackled the boy to the ground.

The man pinned the teenager down and sat on his back.

When Fatima caught up with them, Yusuf was telling the man to get up.

'Phone the police,' the man said.

The teenager was talking in a language Fatima didn't recognise.

'We've got the stuff,' Yusuf said. 'We can let him go.'

'I'm holding him until the police get here,' the man said.

The woman and the estate agent arrived.

'This day,' the estate agent said, out of breath. 'Honestly.'

The four of them argued over what to do. Fatima remained silent.

'He's just a kid. It'll ruin his life,' the woman said, siding with Yusuf.

'We let him go, he'll just rob someone else,' the man said. The estate agent agreed.

The teenager continued to plead.

'Shut it,' the man said, and he slapped the back of his head. The woman was horrified.

'The hell?' Yusuf said, grabbing the man. 'You can't just.'

Yusuf's real voice had returned, and Fatima wondered if the others thought he was now putting on a fake accent.

The estate agent turned to Fatima. 'You've got the deciding vote.'

They all looked at her. During her silence, Yusuf pulled the man off the teenager. The man took out his phone and dialled 999. The teenager ran, leaving everything he'd taken behind.

'Fuck!' the man said. 'See!'

The teenager ran to the edge of the park and gracefully cleared the gates.

Inside the backpack was an old laptop, a few chargers, some shampoo and some food. The handbags were largely empty. One had been filled with loose change that had scattered across the grass when the teenager was tackled. The woman and the estate agent carried the bags back to the house, followed by the man who was describing the events on the phone.

Yusuf and Fatima got on their knees to pick up the fallen coins. As she focussed on the grass, she began to notice a group of ants walking in a line. They moved with such purpose.

Fatima and Yusuf returned to the house. With fresh certainty, she reached out and held his hand. His muddy thumb tapped against hers. The broken TV was gone, as was the estate agent's car. The neighbour's window was closed. They knocked on the door but there was no answer, so they posted the coins through the letterbox, each one landing on the floorboards below and making its own distinct sound.

The Twelfth of Never

———

1741

The sheep was proud of its coat. Then the dark house. The fresh chill of the wind. Days were long, fields open. The dog. The dark house.

*

The carcass arrived. The butcher separated the cuts, hiding a few chops of the rack for himself. He left the intestines to soak.

*

She could tell by the smell that it was soaking day. Sure enough, guts in the kitchen. How she wished she'd married a baker. After soaking, it was scraping, then splitting. After splitting, she and her husband would cut and twist the strands. Soak, dry, twist. Then the horsehair, the grass. Silver and silk. And off to the luthier.

1742

He'd been saving up for the violin so long, he couldn't believe he was actually about to buy one. He handed over his coins and plucked the little strings on the long walk home.

1750

She wanted a freeholder, and he had no land. He sang the song she liked, the one he'd written for her that afternoon by the river.

'It's no use,' she said.

He sang the song at her wedding to the miller's son. He walked home drunk, and sent his fiddle floating down the stream.

1805

Her boy was always asking about things.

'Why is grass green? How come winter is cold? Where did that song come from?'

'My grandfather would sing it while working.' And she took him to what was left of the old watermill and explained how the river used to make grain.

1820

Only one man had a hat. He was nice enough to share it around, and they'd each take a turn in its small shade, as the carriage rolled down the uneven road.

If you were wearing the hat, you had to sing, the old man said. The young man only knew one song, one his mother would sing, her grandfather's song. It felt so nice to have the sun out of his eyes, that he added a verse, and then another. By the time they met the Thames, they all knew the words.

1837

The singer wasn't very good. It was all right if you were just passing through, but working in the shop across the road, it's all she heard. Those three songs on repeat. Then one day he wasn't there and never came back, and she'd have those bloody songs stuck in her head.

1845

He could have sworn he saw her face in the water. Not just the whisky talking. Maybe it was a sign from God, go back, go back. Not that she'd have him. He thought he'd forget her when he arrived and settled down for his new life. But when they hit land and he got a ride out of state and another into Appalachia, and he set his eyes upon his own plot of land, she'd still be there, in his head, in front of him in that little boat, singing that song she liked.

1890

She thought she'd never make it out. Evenings, she'd sit out front and sing, and now and then neighbours might stop by. But this one day a man she's never seen takes pause to listen. He gets to talking to her, and that very night, marches inside and asks her daddy for his blessing. Just like that.

1898

The lady didn't want her singing any Black songs. Before she started the job, the mother taught her good, proper songs to sing to the child. She was supposed to sing while the baby nursed. If the lady cared enough to know, she might ask, of an afternoon, how much did the little one drink? And she'd say, he drank one song, ma'am. He was a hungry one today: three songs.

1921

He saw the advertisement in the daily. Caught a ride down the Mississippi, playing for the fishermen. There was all sorts in the line when he arrived, the building as grand as you could picture. He sang one of his ma's favourites, and the white man sent him through to the next room. Here, he had to put his head in the big brass hole that looked like the end of a trombone, and then sing the song. The machine made ripples in the wax. A record, a real record.

1929

It was her idea, but now she was nervous. He gave her a leg up and then followed her through the window. The factory was chaos; it was shutting that very day. The workers rushed about, and the two of them just walked up to the line, picking up records at random, as many as they could carry.

1950

These days, you got all sorts. Today, it was a beatnik with a big old beard, talked nonstop. He comes in and heads straight for the records. Quite clearly inebriated. About an hour or so later – who spends an hour looking at records? – he comes back with a pile of old 78s. What's a man want with 78s these days? And why so many? He didn't know, didn't care. Money was money.

1963

She was at her wits' end with him. The company needed the jingle yesterday, and here he was setting fire to their music.

'It's no good,' he said, the lighter not working. 'We need to start over.'

She imagined him catching on fire. She put a record on, one of his folk anthologies from the 50s. She dropped the needle in the middle and started to jot down the melody.

'That could work,' he said. 'That could work.'

The ad agency rejected it – it didn't 'scream peanut butter' – and they headed for a drink. They left the sheet music right there on the bar, and any hopes of making it.

*

If the music on the bar wasn't the sign she'd been waiting for, then what was? She hummed the tune, she liked it. There was something in it, she thought. The next day she booked herself a slot at 4th and Mercer. She was going to be a singer.

2020

For once, Umer woke first. He watched Priyanka sleep until it felt
a little creepy, and then read the news. She would tell him off if
he didn't wake her, but he couldn't bring himself to interrupt her.
Especially with how she'd been sleeping. It was nice to just lie there,
to have nothing to do. Things were good. He was blessed. When
the patch of sunlight reached the wall, he put on their song, an
old recording from the 60s that Priyanka found on Spotify. As the
first verse began, she opened her eyes. It was moments like this, he
thought, that memory couldn't do justice. That was the thing, you
couldn't look back and dissect joy, you just had to let it in, a breeze
on a warm morning, eyelashes unfurling, the chorus beginning.

We Move

———

1

WHEN LATA FELT HER PHONE VIBRATE and saw the voice note from David, she didn't even open it. Went back to her book like it was nothing. It was a year since they last spoke, and she was over it. Maybe he'd heard she was coming home. Maybe Auntie Jackie told him about her dropping out.

The coach changed lanes, finally approaching Victoria. Lata looked at the same page so long the ink seemed to shake, words becoming shapes. She'd been on the final chapter for miles. Pretending to read, she watched the TikTok dance compilation the boy next to her was playing. She didn't touch her phone until she'd got off the coach and walked to the underground, where she used it to tap in at the gates. His notification hovered on her home screen. He was still saved in her contacts as Daviddd.

On the tube, she read and reread the same advert until it meant nothing, scratching the tattoo on her left wrist – a soundwave of the opening notes of *The Rapture* – which she'd got a few years ago. As the carriage rattled, she remembered chatting with David, the summer they started making music; they were walking down the canal when, suddenly serious, he said: 'Sound *moves*, man. There were these Tibetan monks, right, on TV, who used music to move stones. No word of a lie, they were making a temple or something up on this cliff and used music to transport the stones up. Had drums and wind instruments and shit and played and chanted a certain distance from the stone. Mum's life, it would start to vibrate, right, the stone, like proper dancing, and then it would lift off the ground and *rise*.'

She'd lost it at the way he said *rise*. He hummed at a pebble, eyes closed, fingers at his temples and she tossed it into the canal. Ripples in the Grand Union as they levitated rocks, leaves, an empty bottle of Lucozade, David's laughter rising in pitch.

His voice was noticeably low in the recording, now that it was playing – her data returned when she passed White City – dropping the way it did when he was trying to impress. It had always wavered around Lata – David oscillating between the person he projected and the person he was, the boy she'd known since nursery.

'Hey, so yeah. Hope you're good and that. I heard you was coming back to London, and I was just wondering if you might be up for working together again. I've been booked for Fire in the Booth and want my best writer on this one. But no stress. Mad how long it's been, still.'

She drafted a response in Notes.

Its a freestyle make it up
Your taking liberties sending this
Air me for a year and this is all you have to say?
You think youd at least call

She looked up from her phone, her reflection stretched in the curved glass. A grown woman getting worked up on high school drama? She wasn't about that life. If her teenage self could see her now – *Allow it. Allow him.*

Deciding not to respond, she tried to distract herself. She searched for the levitating monks, surprised it was a thing – you never knew with David. The levitation had been captured on film, but the reels had been classified, the negatives left to rot. But other sites said that was a fake story, a stupid conspiracy.

It wasn't until she got on the bus and arrived in Southall that she began to think about her mum, and what she would say about quitting her PhD. Auntie Jackie said Mum would take it fine, but in the month since she dropped out, Lata had been unable to tell her. The windows shook as the engine turned over, the Broadway passing in stops and starts, the smells of steamed sweetcorn and fried jalebi rising with exhaust fumes. Pulling up outside Nationwide, she watched a group of schoolkids heckle a pastor riffing off Revelations: 'The great vibration,' he repeated into his megaphone, 'it's coming.' The kids got on the bus, oversized blazers and short ties. Straight to the backseats, they chatted over music someone was playing on a phone. Sounded like Chronicle. It would be simple, Lata decided, getting off at her stop and dragging her suitcase down the road to her house: she would just tell her mum it was over.

2

Meena watched the silhouette of her daughter through the front door's frosted glass. Lata hadn't put her key in the door, hadn't knocked. Just stood there, captured in fog. Meena would have opened the door, but that would have given away the fact she'd nothing better to do than wait for her daughter in the hallway like some dog.

She remembered when she and Lata had their own secret knock. Lata had to know it was really her behind the door, not an imposter. They had a secret everything back then, a handshake, their own language. Meena had encouraged the made-up talking, having heard from teachers that Lata wasn't speaking in class. For the most part, the invented language was English backwards, but like the handshake, it grew increasingly complex. Got to the point that it'd take so long to form a sentence that a simple conversation would last an evening and they'd turn in having said almost nothing. Meena couldn't remember any of their words now. She wondered if Lata could.

The language lasted a few months, and then there was the invisible ink, which had been fun at first – little notes in lunchboxes, a birthday card only the two of them could read – but then Meena made the mistake of passing the black light scanner over one of Lata's schoolbooks and found the words: bullshit, cock, etc. Jackie told her not to read into it, kids tested boundaries, 'they need to know the edge of things'. It wasn't so much the rudeness of the words that worried Meena, it was that they were so out of character. Her Lata was in Gifted & Talented, but here was this whole other world, her own daughter suddenly a stranger to her. How glad she was that things had worked out. That she could tell everyone at the office that her child was doing a *doctorate*.

Finally, Lata unlocked the door.

'You're disappearing,' Meena said, hugging her. 'You might want to get freshened up before we eat. Looking tired.'

Meena had planned a secret welcome-home dinner and invited Jackie and David. Lata had always loved surprises.

3

Lata was missing her chance. Her mum was already repeating a story she'd told her over the phone – some woman she'd met at Lavani class who claimed to have known a famous playback singer. Lata nodded along, failing to find an opening. She'd kept the lie up a month, she could keep it going a little longer. She decided she'd come clean about dropping out over dinner and headed up to her room to unpack.

There were pictures up in the house now, old photos that had spent decade in albums. Mum must have spent an evening sorting through them, deciding what to display: Lata in front of the Colosseum, the Eiffel Tower, black-and-white portraits of Aaji and Ajoba, a signed photo of David performing at the BRITs, a photo of Mum and Auntie Jackie holding Lata and David at one of the Southall Black Sisters demonstrations, Mum's sign cropped off by the frame to read 'No Silence'. Their mums were members of SBS, and Lata and David would play together at the meetings and occasional marches. While she couldn't remember what they'd been protesting, and wouldn't have understood as a child, the feeling of chanting in those crowds stuck with her, different voices becoming one. At an anniversary gathering on the Broadway, their small group had repeated one slogan: 'Our Tradition: Struggle Not Submission!' and Lata remembered changing the words: 'Owl Transmission: Suck All Snot Magicians!'

She told this to her ex, Deep, during her undergrad, when he questioned her for one of his psychology modules. He'd phoned her mum beforehand to elicit the key events of her childhood, and then asked Lata about them. They discussed the break-in at the house, the intruder in the doorway, talked about results day, when she got straight As, and then he asked her about the time she got lost in a shopping centre. She hadn't thought about it in years, but slowly the memory returned. They were protesting on Ealing Broadway, and Lata and David, lost in the crowd, sneaked off to the shops. They wandered around until an old woman alerted security. A call was put out on the Tannoy – it was surreal to hear her own name coming from the speakers.

Deep got a good mark for the coursework – it turned out the shopping centre story had never happened and that he'd managed to plant the memory in her by asking about it. The more she thought about the fake memory, the realer it felt, and new details would emerge. She could remember the brand of the old woman's handbag. One night, visiting David's new penthouse, he went on about the day they handed out demos by Ealing Town Hall, and all Lata could think was that was where the police had taken them to wait for their mums.

Lata had seen some of those demos go for three figures online. She and David had burned actual CDs after uploading the mixtape to SoundCloud, and he'd drawn a logo of his stage name for the cover art: *Sketch*.

The music began a year earlier. Lata had thought David's whole rapping thing was an extension of what they used to do when they were kids, when they'd do dance routines in front of their mums. David would rap other people's lyrics while she played the backing track to 'Bitch Don't Kill My Vibe' again and again. Bored, she started to jot down her own mock lyrics. She was trying to be funny, but when David read them, he insisted she write more. One moment it was joking around and the next it was something real, which, Lata now knew, was always the way with him.

She enjoyed writing for him. She was the person behind the mask; he was the shell. He'd call her at night with ideas and she'd DM him the lyrics. They decided to create a character, modelling Sketch after their favourite rapper, MF DOOM. It was Lata who introduced David to DOOM; they'd thought they were so edgy listening to him, rolling their eyes at the mumble rap that was popular at the time. They saw him live a few weeks after David first went studio: DOOM showed up late, trademark mask glistening in the spotlight. He got a few bars into 'Beef Rap' before the crowd started to boo, calling him an imposter. The impersonator walked offstage, and the real DOOM walked on, except that wasn't really him either. By the third song, there were four men in masks on stage, one of whom might have been him. Lata and David sang along, their voices one.

When she watched David's own shows from the wings, a few years later, and saw her own lyrics coming out of fans' mouths, she felt a sisterly pride. She took it upon herself to protect him, especially when women would flock to him after the shows. It always took him a while to come down from the high of performing, and he easily made bad decisions. With all those people looking for Sketch, she didn't want David to lose himself. But then it happened. It was after his set at the Village Underground when, drunk off the energy of the crowd, and the sponsored vodka in the green room, he moved to her. It was their last night together before she moved to Manchester for her PhD. They were on their way to afters. It was cold and she was shaking. He put his arm around her and something in his gaze altered, shifted register. He leaned in, suddenly real.

'I didn't mean nothing,' he said, after she'd drawn away.

She didn't know what to think and ended up saying something that was so out of place that the words seemed to belong to a different person. 'Sorry bro, it's just—'

She was glad he didn't hear her. She followed him down the steps into Apocalypse. The bouncer stamped a mushroom cloud on her hand. The club was modelled after old fallout shelters. Fake news footage of the wasteland above ground played on loop on vintage TV sets. The DJ, wearing a gas mask, stood shrouded in smoke, her t-shirt glowing green in the black light. The bar was lined with rows of canned goods. Lata ordered shots, not wanting the kiss to change anything, but David had already disappeared, lost in mist, and she drank alone. Her life could have been very comfortable, she thought, if she'd decided to kiss him back. They'd probably be good together. A lot of his fans probably dreamed of a moment like that, outside. But she just couldn't see him like that. He'd been in her life for so long. She ordered more drinks and they eventually met on the dancefloor, both of them off their faces, only half joking as they pulled some of the moves they'd practised as kids, when they'd perform for their mums – brother and sister. She did the steps to their 'Tujhe Dekha To' routine. She'd wanted so badly to perform it at their talent show when they were kids – they had a dance for every song in DDLJ – but he'd have killed her if she ever mentioned the dancing at school.

'It's like that, yeah?' he said, recognising the routine. He went up to the DJ to put in a request and soon house gave way to filmi. Violins, tabla. After the opening notes, she realised David had got the song wrong. 'Kuch Kuch Hota Hai' came on, Udit Narayan's voice filling the club: '*something is happening*'. It didn't matter, they danced and danced, everyone else in the club backing dancers, a beat away from moving into formation and falling into step behind them.

She got less self-conscious when she was drunk, but more self-centred. This, she thought now, was the reason she didn't clock the shift in David's mood until they were in the Uber home. He was staring straight ahead, so at first, she thought he was talking to the driver when he spoke:

'We need to learn to be our own people.'

The words ran through her head now, back in her old bedroom, a year later. She couldn't remember what she'd said back. The whole exchange had been condensed to that one line, which came back to her each time she saw Sketch. Which was often. The algorithm knew they had a history; he was always appearing in her suggested. She'd get targeted ads for his tour, or his merch, which she'd actually seen one of her first-year students wearing in her Old English seminar. He looked out at her from billboards, and often, walking through shops, or venturing out to bars, she'd hear her lyrics and his voice. Sometimes he was in the news. The *Daily Mail* had broken a story about an alleged affair between David and the dancer in the music video for 'Waiting for the Drop Like' who was apparently married. In the video, she gives Sketch a lap dance, but as the song goes on, her moves become increasingly erratic, and she starts to shake as if possessed. The audio glitches and Sketch sounds like he's speaking tongues. Lata had watched a fifteen-minute video explaining the Illuminati symbolism in the song. Five minutes in, they play Sketch's vocals backwards, trying to reveal the secret messages. She'd wanted to forward it to David but stopped herself. It was on him to break the silence.

Lata heard her name. Her mum was calling her down to help with dinner.

'Tell me all about it, then,' her mum said. 'How's the research? The teaching?'

This was her chance. It was here, and it was passing.

4

Lata started to talk about her thesis and Meena tried to pay attention: heteroglossia, the Lyric I. The academic stuff was all over Meena's head; Lata always used to take her school questions to Jackie. While she didn't understand what her daughter was saying, Meena did enjoy the sound of it, and she wished Lata's Aaji could see her now; she was always on about education when Meena was growing up. She'd come home from the foundry, hands seized up with that tremor, and lecture Meena about the importance of school. Meena would pretend to listen, the words washing over her. But one speech stood out, even now, and Meena often thought about it when she cooked and saw her mother's miniature Nataraja replica statue on her kitchen windowsill. She could remember it shaking in her mother's trembling hands as she told Meena about the Ananda Tandav, the Dance of Bliss. The little statue showed Shiva, the Nataraja, Lord of Dancers, dancing in a ring of fire. In one hand, he holds an hourglass-shaped drum, from which the first vibrations of the universe originated. In another, he holds a flame, representing transformation.

'The dance of bliss is the basis of existence,' her mother said, in Marathi. 'Everything is constantly moving between creation and destruction. Each atom in an endless dance, vibrating. Srishti, sthiti, samhara, tirobhava, anugraha.'

'Did I ever tell you about this?' Meena said, now that Lata had stopped talking. She pointed to the small statue on the windowsill.

'Dance of bliss. Creation. Destruction. Everything beginning and ending with a dance,' Lata said. 'Yeah, more than once. Why are we making so much food? There's no way we can eat all this.'

'Because my daughter has come home.'

'I'm not a guest, Mum.'

'You are when you don't visit for nine months.'

'It's not been that long.'

It had. Jackie had reminded her of that when convincing Meena to come on her trip at lunch over a month ago.

'I can't just up and leave,' Meena had said. 'What about Lata?'

'She's an adult. She's got her own life. And that's the point. It's our turn. Time for us to have our own lives.'

When they were in their twenties, two single mothers raising only children, Meena and Jackie used to make pretend plans to see the world. In their fictional lives, they'd go as soon as the kids left home. It was all talk. But then David made a fortune overnight, and Jackie's unemployment from the library closure became early retirement. Meena told her she'd think about it. But she and Jackie had barely spoken in the last month. Jackie would be expecting an answer at dinner.

Meena could feel the meal getting away from her. She couldn't remember if she'd already added salt to the dal, and she was sure there wasn't enough lamb. She looked over at her daughter, taking too much ginger off with the peel. Lata would probably encourage her to take the trip. What was three months away from her mother? At some point they stopped wanting you and at another they stopped needing you. Lata was eying her phone, something off. Probably a boy.

'Everything all right?'

Lata didn't respond. Maybe she didn't hear? Meena turned back to the stove. She knew nothing about Lata's love life. She could still remember with vivid intensity the time she found out that Lata had told Jackie about her first boyfriend, Arun, before she told her. She'd been livid, did Lata really think she was someone who would disapprove? Wasn't long ago that Meena was a teen-ager lying to her own parents. On Wednesdays, she'd sneak off to daytime discos, hiding an outfit in her bag, telling her mother that she had to stay late at college. She'd queue up with her girlfriends outside the club after lunch and beeline it to the loos when the doors opened to unbraid her hair, change into her white clothes and put on the jewellery she'd nicked from her mother's vanity. Inside, the windows were blacked out and when the bhangra played and everyone danced, you'd never have known it was the middle of the afternoon in the middle of England.

The last Wednesday of college, they made up a fake school trip and took a coach all the way from Birmingham to Bradford to see DJ Radical Sista at Queen's Hall. The dhol from the speakers whipped her heartbeat into a frenzy, ripples running through her blood. She couldn't understand the lyrics, most of them in Punjabi, so the singing itself became more fully music, the voice an instrument. She felt most within her body when she danced, as if it was what her limbs had been specifically designed to do. The men spread their arms out in the air, bodies drifting through clouds of cologne and fake smoke. Shaking bodies almost touching, then touching, a brush of her cheek on one of theirs, a hand on her lower back. There was a flash – someone taking a photo that would later get developed back in Brum and do the rounds, increasingly distorted copies passed between Gurdwaras, Mandirs and Mosques throughout the Midlands, until one found its way into her mother's shaking hands. She was married a few months later and moved to London.

Two months before her divorce, Meena met Jackie. She'd taken Lata to the library to get out of the house, and Jackie had seen the bruise. She slipped a leaflet to Meena, and they met again at an SBS meeting a week later. Lata was making her first sounds and babbled away at David. The kids were the same age. They arranged a playdate.

Lata and David gave them the perfect reason to see each other. But it had become harder to stay close since the kids left. Now when they met, it was at Jackie's posh White City house, heading out for tiny portions of sushi, or to look at abstract paintings, or watch plays with no singing and no dancing. This one time, Jackie took her to a spa where all you did was lie in a tank in the dark – the things the rich spent their money on. To be fair, it was in the tank that Meena had properly thought about things. In their twenties they saw their kids as holding them down, but with hindsight Meena saw Lata and David as holding them together. Now that she thought about it, she hadn't really felt like she'd missed anything, not talking to Jackie this last month. They were their best selves around the kids. If she had to think back to the last genuinely good time she'd had with Jackie, it was still centred around the children – Meena had taken Lata's ticket to a taping of a talk show David was appearing on. She and Jackie sat in the front row. David performed a song at the end. It was a new style for him, not like the stuff on his first album, where he rapped so fast you could hardly make out a word. Meena asked Lata if she'd caught the performance on TV, surprised she hadn't, and told her to get it up on her phone.

5

The song had Lata dying. David on a triplet flow? You couldn't write it. The two of them used to joke about mumble rap, and here he was barely forming words, ad libs and all. No thoughts, just vibes. It was even worse when you could hear the lyrics; David didn't know shit about food and country, but here he was acting road for a crowd who likely couldn't understand him. But up there in his trademark cap, it was Sketch, not David. The character had become a caricature.

She scrolled through the comments. Most were positive, but there were a few that said he'd sold out, gone American. Some were comparing him to artists Lata hadn't even heard of. She'd been out of the loop with music for the last year, her short-lived PhD passing to the sound of slowed & reverb instrumentals.

During her year in Manchester, she listened to the same lo-fi playlist each day at her spot in the library, stuck in the same research rut. Her thesis, she soon realised, was too ambitious; she was trying to outline the influence of Bede's *Ecclesiastical History of the English People* on the prose poetry of interwar modernist SG, with the aim of showing that the speaker of SG's 'VI' was based on Bede's Cædmon. She'd learned about Cædmon, the earliest-known English poet, during her undergrad, and remembered David reading 'Cædmon's hymn' out loud and laughing, 'Nine K a year for this, yeah?' In Bede's story, Cædmon, an illiterate cowherd, left a feast one night because he was embarrassed about not knowing any songs. When he arrived home, he was visited by an angel:

'Cædmon, sing me something.' Then he answered and said: 'I do not know how to sing and for that reason I went out from this feast and went hither, because I did not know how to sing at all.' Again he said, he who was speaking with him: 'Nevertheless, you must sing.' Then he said: 'What must I sing?' Said he: 'Sing to me of the first Creation.' When he received this answer, then he began immediately to sing in praise of God the Creator verses and words which he had never heard ...

The main reason for Lata's slow progress was that each time she decided on an interpretation of one of SG's poems, the meaning would seem to shift, and her line of enquiry would lead to a dead end. SG's writing was so dense and many-voiced as to read as code, which is why, Lata thought, critics seemed to focus on aspects of her biography, rather than the work itself. Focussing so deeply on her close-readings, and spending so much time alone in the library, Lata found the stress of David and the music recede, as if it belonged to some other, distant self. But then her advisor forwarded her the news about SG and it all came back.

SG's only collection was published long after her untimely death, when the poems were discovered by a publisher in the 70s, along with a collection of her diaries. A recluse, SG had never considered publishing the poems herself. Apparently, a descendent of the publisher had found one of SG's missing diaries in her attic. It covered the year in which the poems were said to be composed. According to the diary, SG's husband had suffered a stroke which damaged the Wernicke's area of his cerebral cortex, resulting in what was now known as Fluent Aphasia. To quote SG, 'it seemed to me as if he had suddenly begun to speak in tongues.' Lata searched 'fluent aphasia' in a separate tab. It was a speech disorder in which patients retain the ability to speak but can lose the ability to make sense. SG's husband would talk with his usual intonations and speed, but the words he spoke no longer matched those that he thought. 'I have taken to noting down his speech so as to better understand it,' SG wrote, 'but I find myself *[unintelligible]*. The doctors say that time can heal.'

Apparently, the publisher had found the diaries at an auction and thought the abstracted speech was similar to what was passing as poetry in those days. He copied sections out as a joke to show his friends, but they liked them. He was soon credited with unearthing a lost voice of literature. He hid the diary.

Lata closed the article. She left the library, surprised by the daylight and, waiting for the bus, watched a group of Hare Krishnas sing and dance down Oxford Road. She thought about phoning David.

Her advisor thought this dramatic shift in context would electrify her essay, give it a real sense of urgency. Lata left his office hours and thought about phoning David again. She even drafted a message to send to him. But when she opened his contact and saw the empty chat history – she'd deleted all their messages a few months back, when it was clear he didn't want to speak to her – she stopped herself. He obviously wanted space. His status said, 'last seen five minutes ago', and she wondered who he might have been talking to and about what.

She thought about calling her mum but knew that her advice would be to stick with it, *we never give up, we keep moving forward*. Lata knew how her mum bragged about her PhD, as if it were her own accomplishment. No, instead, she ended up dialling the one person she thought might understand her: Auntie Jackie.

'You have to do you,' Auntie Jackie said, when Lata told her she was thinking of dropping out. 'Every ending is a beginning.'

Auntie Jackie agreed not to say anything to her mum or David. Lata said she'd tell them herself. But days passed in Manchester and she didn't tell her mum. The longer she left it the harder it was to bring up. She didn't leave her room, realising that after months in Manchester, she had no one she could really call a friend. Most of her friends in London she'd met through David. Maybe he was right, they needed to learn to function without each other. Having him by her side whenever she needed him had stunted her growth. She didn't feel fully herself without him.

Even at her lowest, the algorithm taunted her. She was listening to her usual instrumental playlist while looking for jobs, when she was suggested a 'Genius: Lyrics Explained' interview David had done for one of the songs she'd written. She spent an embarrassing amount of time in the comments section; fans were raving about the double meanings and word play. There was one comment from someone they'd gone to school with: 'real ones been on this since prom ifykyk.'

The Sixth Form prom was David's first show. The theme was masquerade ball, though Lata's mask fell off and got trampled in what became a mosh pit, hers one of the only bare faces in the frenzied crowd. Her favourite song got two reloads, everyone in their year losing it at the drop of the type beat David had worked Saturdays at Next to afford. David jumped into the tightly packed crowd, floating on the surface of their outstretched hands. Lata told her date, Arun, that she'd written the lyrics.

'You what?' he shouted back, gesturing to his ear.

She signalled to forget about it and went back to pretending to dance. Arun was the first and last person she'd told about the ghost-writing. When David got his record deal, she had to sign an NDA. Written in indecipherable legalese, she signed it without really reading. She got a lump sum that seemed a lot at the time and would never have thought to push for royalties. She didn't resent the money he made; she was by his side through it all, would come along when he went radio, would sit backstage at his shows. Throughout her undergrad in London, her motives revolved around his – hard not to get gassed from bottomless champagne in the VIP section, the glitter of paparazzi flashes as they cut lines at whatever clubs they wanted. Her stories did numbers and she gained hundreds of followers. But stuck in the library last year, she'd watched them gradually disappear.

Lata opened Twitter now that she was done with the ginger and almost laughed, the algorithm fucking with her.

Sketch was trending.

'Are you sure everything's okay?' her mum asked. 'Who are you talking to?'

'No one,' Lata said.

'Right.'

She looked up from her phone. 'David's trending on Twitter.'

'Is that good?'

Lata scrolled through the tweets, piecing together what had happened. 'This rapper, Chronicle, he's just released a diss track and he's sending for Sketch.'

The song was called 'No Cap'. Lata was about to click the link when something exploded outside, and the Nataraja dropped off the windowsill and cracked on the floor.

6

The sound had David shook, still. Stopped the traffic dead, everyone in the street looking up for a sign from above.

'What was that?' his manager said, on speakerphone. 'You okay?'

'It's calm,' David said, looking through the sunroof. Nothing seemed out of place. Maybe a car backfired? 'All good.'

'Right, so as I was saying, I really think the best course is to respond quickly. Come out guns blazing within twenty-four hours. This close to the next single, it'll do wonders for numbers. This whole thing will only work in our favour.'

'I told you I'm not getting involved.'

'Did you read the case studies I sent?' his manager said. The lights changed and everyone moved on with their day. 'David, streams almost doubled.'

'Look, I'm not getting involved.'

'I don't – how about you let the guys come up with something, see what you think?'

The writers would be gassed to work on a diss track, getting to say anything they wanted about Chronicle with no consequences. The whole thing was bait. A few months ago, Chronicle had asked him to do a feature on his upcoming release. David had refused – he refused all collabs – and now he was being called fake. Story old as time, an artist facing irrelevancy taking their insecurities out on someone younger and more successful.

He looked at the time, his mum's appointment ending in forty minutes. He knew he should turn back, but he carried on heading towards Auntie Meena's as if he were doing a trial run for later. He could still pull out, he thought, looking through the tinted windows, approaching his and Lata's old route to school. Here was the corner shop where they'd get sweets in the mornings and there was XFC where they'd get the value box on the way home. Coming up was the lamppost Lata had walked into when trying to steal his chips. That was probably the hardest he'd ever laughed. Every time they passed it from then on, he'd grab her arm as if he were saving her from a collision. Never got old.

His manager continued, saying that fans would believe Chronicle if he didn't respond.

'Let them. It's mostly true.'

'David, come on. This is the dancer thing all over again. Saying nothing is as good as a confirmation.'

'All right,' David said, finally making a U-turn. 'In a bit.'

He hung up and headed back to the floatation centre. When he was in London, he always picked his mum up from her isolation sessions. It was on the way back from the centre a few weeks ago that she told him Lata was coming home for the summer. That's when he fully deeped it: a year. A whole year without her.

He'd dialled his spiritual advisor as soon as his mum had left the car.

'I crossed the line, man. I know that. I should never have made a move.'

His advisor, as usual, stayed quiet. They only ever spoke on the phone, and David often wondered what he looked like, what he did during their calls. David pictured him sitting in lotus position, hovering above the ground.

'I don't even remember it. This was back when I was drinking. It was a blur. In the morning all I could remember was trying to kiss her. Made me feel sick. She's like a sister to me.'

'Did you tell her that?'

'I figured she'd want space. Wanted to respect boundaries and that.' He waited for his advisor to say something, and then carried on. 'She was going Manchester, I was going on tour. I don't know. We'd never really been apart, I thought she was probably enjoying that. Few weeks later was the Mercury. I couldn't even get excited about it, I just wanted to call her.'

'But you didn't.'

'It doesn't make sense. Like, twenty years over one mistake?'

'Silence can mean any number of things.'

'All that time together. I don't think I even wanted – she was always stopping me getting with other girls. I thought maybe that's why. I don't know. It's why I stopped with the drink. I think things just got confused.'

'And now you're clear.'

He thought he was. But this morning, it had taken ten minutes to decide what to wear. He was nervous at the thought of the dinner, of her feeling ambushed – she'd always hated surprises – and he figured it would be best to get ahead of it, to message her. Then the question of what the fuck to say. Auntie Meena would kill him if he mentioned the dinner. How to talk about the kiss, the year of nothing? He decided to talk about the music. But his mind went blank as soon as he pressed record. For some reason, he mentioned Fire in the Booth, even though he'd turned it down. He listened to it back – didn't matter how many streams he got, he still couldn't stand the sound of his voice, high and thin. He kept the screen open until her status changed to 'Active Now'. The blue ticks eventually appeared to say she'd seen the message. He could hear his pulse.

He clicked off the chat. To distract himself, he relistened to 'No Cap'. He just couldn't get offended by it. All of Chronicle's insults were aimed at Sketch, a fucking made-up character. He remembered watching Chronicle's freestyles on repeat when he was a kid; Chronicle had done Fire in the Booth three times in three years, and in each one, it seemed like he would never run out of words, as if they were simply passing through him. He reopened the chat, Lata's status: 'last seen today at 15.35'.

He scrolled up the chat history, their old messages perfectly preserved. Half the texts just said 'outside' – she never used the buzzer when she came round. There were lots of memes that she'd shared, some demos he'd wanted her opinion on. Even though they used to see each other all the time, they were constantly messaging. He could remember their snap streak at school, hundreds of days long. At some point, keeping the streak going became more important than their actual conversation, so they'd just send each other blank photos with nonsense captions.

He continued to scroll, wondering how long it would take to get back to them at 17, Lata messaging him her lyrics. Back then, David had been putting everything into writing, but nothing worked. And there she was coming up with a sixteen with no effort. It had pissed him off. He'd wanted to tell her that the lyrics were bad but didn't have it in him to offend her. Reluctantly, he asked if she could write some more, and a year later they had enough for a mixtape. Feeling guilty, he'd often justify the situation, telling himself it was a collaboration, that she got everything she knew about music from him anyway, he was the one who would find new artists to listen to, he was the one who came up with the concept of it all. The only times he was really convinced were when he was on stage. He entered a kind of trance when he performed, finally getting out of his head. He didn't know how to describe the feeling, other than to say it felt like living purely in the present tense, the past turning over behind you and the future a blank page. He'd snap out of it if he saw someone in the crowd not feeling it. Like at his first show, crowd surfing at prom, he'd glimpsed Lata's face in the crowd, talking to that wasteman, breaking the spell.

He arrived at the floatation centre with a few minutes to spare. Parked up, he eyed the pub across the road, tapping a rhythm on the steering wheel. He put his cap on and decided to go into the centre early. The receptionist grinned – she'd asked for a selfie the first time he'd come, and he tried to remember her name as he approached the desk, and then read it on her badge. She beamed when he said it.

'Course I remembered,' he said. 'Am I good to wait inside?'

He sat on the bench opposite the row of doors, waiting for his mum to emerge. It was his spiritual advisor who first suggested the isolation therapy. He'd told David to use the time to set his intention and his direction. 'The power of prayer,' he said, 'is that you hear nothing back. It forces you to listen to yourself.'

He checked his phone, 'sonic boom' all over his timeline. Apparently, the explosion he'd heard was the sound of a fighter jet going supersonic, chasing down an unidentified plane. 'Sketch' and 'Chronicle' were also trending – he muted them both.

7

Jackie was seeing things. Purple masses pulsing in the impossible dark. She reached out her left hand to confirm they were fake, but her arm was lost to her, it was gone. She tried to find it with her right, but they missed each other in the air, floating figments, her body a vapour. The salt water she was lying on was the exact temperature of her skin, of the air, so the borders between the three became blurred, her body without edges, porous. Thoughts drifted out into the tank, no longer hers, like, how long had she been here? Impossible to say: time had no purchase. The whole centre existed out of time to her; she had a standing slot each week and when she arrived at reception, the binaural background music playing from the hidden surround sound would be at the exact same point in its cycle, as if each time she arrived, she'd never left.

The tanks were entirely soundproof, and when she'd been immersed for a certain amount of time – five minutes, thirty? – she would slowly be able to tune into what she thought of as her internal music. She'd tried and failed to describe the sensation to Meena, who clearly thought she was losing it. She could hear melodies from her childhood surfacing, her father returning from work and asking her to fetch his guitar once the table was cleared. The percussion of her mother washing dishes accompanying him as he played his palm wine music. Sometimes he picked up the tempo and strayed into highlife; he couldn't keep from smiling when he played, and neither could Jackie, sometimes joining in and singing, which he'd encouraged even after she'd been dropped by choir and had to watch all her friends sing 'We Shall Overcome' without her. She remembered the occasions when they'd restring the guitar, walking home from the music shop, Jackie wearing the coiled-up strings like golden bracelets. She'd given the guitar to David when he started doing music at school. It came home the next day with a Nike tick sharpied under the pickguard. He gave it up after a few weeks, slowly becoming the boy she'd always feared.

When she'd first found out she was having a son, she'd been filled with a kind of dread: how to bring a boy into the world without him becoming one of those men? She'd always imagined herself with a daughter. After her first ultrasound, she'd bought a special microphone that attached to her bump and would talk to him; the vibrations, the packaging promised, seeping through the walls of the womb. She'd tell him about her day, would read to him from the stack of books she'd taken out before her leave. She told everyone that his first kick was in response to the words of Audre Lorde. She felt a deep relief when he took to Lata. Surely men like his father didn't spend so much time dancing and lip syncing as children.

Meena told her she was worrying about nothing. Jackie could

see her clearly now, the two of them watching those Indian dramas while the kids played.

'Okay, so, in ten years they'll be eighteen and we'll be untethered. Where are we going first?'

'Italy. I've always wanted to go.'

That answer changed as Meena and Lata actually went on holidays: Italy, Spain, France. Meena's HR job paid well. When they went away, Jackie tried to keep David entertained in the flat, sometimes secretly taking him over to Meena's house so he could play on Lata's Xbox. She enjoyed those phantom visits, all that space. One day, when Meena and Lata were in Paris, Jackie decided that they'd stay the night. David had been so happy, spent the whole time on that wrestling game. They ordered takeout, and Jackie felt almost giddy when she answered the door, the delivery man thinking the house was hers, no idea she was an imposter. She flicked through one of Lata's schoolbooks in the morning, rows of neat writing, methodical working out. Lata reminded Jackie of what she was like as a child; she was reading way past her age, taking books from the library that David would never think to pick up. He just wasn't interested. By then, he'd stopped all the singing and dancing. If you could get him talking it was wrestling.

And then it happened. She was at work, processing returns, when she got the call from the Head. She could see David's thirteen-year-old face now, floating above her, bloodied hands and a bruise on his left cheek, beating purple. A crab doesn't give birth to a bird. The world was in him. The Head tried to mediate a conversation between the boys, but David gave nothing but mumbles, fragments of sentences: 'He stepped to me.'

After leaving the floatation room and showering, she found David waiting in the hall, wearing his cap indoors. On the way to the car, he told her about Chronicle. She couldn't believe anyone would make a whole song just to insult her son.

'Do you want me to take him?' she said. 'Nobody speaks to my boy like that and gets away with it.'

He smiled. 'I think we're good, Mum.'

While he drove them to Meena's, she looked up this Chronicle person. She read a few articles. People were so horrible.

David played her some new instrumentals he'd been sent and asked her what she thought. She knew a lot of fans didn't like the new direction Sketch was taking. She had a burner account on Twitter so that she could like tweets about Sketch secretly without embarrassing David. She'd logged in when he premiered his new single, 'We Move', on the talk show. A lot of people preferred the old stuff.

'I'm not sure it's very you,' she said.

They approached Meena's. The house that had once looked so large seemed to have shrunk. Jackie hadn't met up with Meena since Lata called her about dropping out and made her promise not to tell anyone. And the updates to their planned itinerary that she'd messaged Meena had been met with lukewarm responses. The only real conversation they'd had in a month was about planning the dinner. She texted Meena now to let her know they were outside and Meena opened the door, finger at her lips. They walked down the hallway to the kitchen. Lata was speechless when she saw her.

'My girl!' Jackie said, hugging her. 'You're looking thin, are you eating?'

'Auntie,' Lata said, eventually. 'No, yeah, I'm good. I just – how are you? How's everything?'

'Where's David?' Meena said.

Jackie looked around. He was still in the hallway.

8

'What you saying?' David said, when Lata joined him on the sofa. 'How's uni?'

'You'd like Manchester.'

'I was up there for a few shows.'

'I saw.'

'You came?'

'Turns out I'm much less likely to come without free tickets.'

'I would've given them to you.'

'Right.'

'What? I would. Not like you asked.'

She nodded. He looked away. The room hadn't changed. Part of him wanted to turn the Xbox on, load up *SmackDown Vs Raw.*

'Guessing you've heard the whole Chronicle thing,' she said, after a while.

'All I'm hearing about.'

'I thought you'd be in the studio right now.'

'I'm not responding.'

'Really?'

'Yeah. I mean they've got the guys on it, but–'

'Is that the team behind "We Move"?'

'It is.'

She made the ad lib sounds from the hook.

'Rah. It's like that, yeah?'

'It is.'

'I knew you'd hate it.'

'Is that why you were asking about Fire in the Booth?'

He thought about telling her that had been a lie. 'Yeah. And I guess I missed working with you.'

'Working.'

'You know what I mean.'

Another pause. 'Say what you want about the new sound,' he said, 'but that song alone has easily paid for Mum's trip.'

'Trip?'

'You know, she's going travelling with your mum. They were always on about it.'

She took a moment to take that in. 'Yeah,' she said. 'We used to make plans for a massive house party when they were gone.'

She sounded different. Like her 'yes, miss,' voice from school had become permanent. Never ceased to amaze him, the way she'd switch when talking to teachers compared to how she'd speak at break. He'd gone back to their school a few months ago to give a talk. He worked with some music students to come up with an arrangement of a song off *The Rapture*. Drums, guitars, backing singers. Was even this one kid who traded bars with him – the whole school lost it. Bare memories came back to him in that hall; staring at GCSE art pieces on the walls during speeches, the sound of a hundred pages turning at once at the start of an exam, clapping for Lata as she picked up yet another award. Then he remembered the time they made that white woman cry in assembly. She'd come to give a talk on elocution. It was a charity initiative to level the playing field for interviews. When she asked questions, some boys answered in fake freshie accents and got a big laugh. David put his hand up and joined in. The woman politely asked him to repeat his question – everyone was in bits. He'd looked around all smug before catching Lata's eye, one of the only people not laughing. Twisted something in his stomach, that look, as it did now.

'You remember that time I got in that fight at school?' he said.

'Not really.'

'Well, I've been thinking about it. What happened was I was walking down this corridor, right, the long one in Block B. Just minding my own. And there's this guy walking the other way, but on the same side of the hall. I carry on, expecting him to move to one side, to make room. And the thing is, he's expecting me to be the one that moves for him, and he just carries on. I think he was in the year above. There's no one else around. We're getting closer and I get this weird feeling that something might be on. I size him up and that, know I can take him. But I'm still thinking, at the last minute, this guy's gonna step to one side, cos there's no way in hell at this point that I would. But he keeps coming and I keep going and next thing we're fighting.'

She looked at him. 'You saying that's us?'

'I guess. Except, I'm now the kind of guy that wants to step to one side.'

'What if I want to fight?'

'Come at me, sis.'

She threw a cushion at his head. That was a good sign, that had to be a good sign. He threw the cushion back at her. Another pause.

'Do you ever think: would we have been friends if it weren't for our mums?' Lata said.

That twist in the stomach.

'I don't know, I don't really analyse like that.'

'Right.'

'But I do. Yeah, I do.'

Auntie Meena arrived with the food. The dining table was pushed up against the wall, as it had been for years, so they all sat on the same side, facing the same way. Man, he'd missed Auntie's cooking.

9

The food was blander than usual, Jackie thought. She'd poured three glasses from the bottle she'd bought. Lata had already finished hers. Helping in the kitchen, Jackie had realised that Meena still didn't know about Lata quitting. Jackie tried to give Lata a look, but she didn't get the hint.

'It's delicious, Auntie,' David said.

'So, Lata,' Jackie said, cutting him off. 'How's the PhD?'

If looks could kill. Lata finished another glass before speaking. 'I quit.'

'For real?' David said.

'Sorry I didn't quite – did you say quit?' Meena said.

Lata gave what sounded like a rehearsed speech. Jackie didn't really listen, watching, instead for Meena's reaction. Meena and Lata talked, and Jackie and David ate. And then Meena asked a question.

'Did you know?'

'It was only a few weeks ago,' Jackie said.

The look of surprise on Meena's face made Jackie realise she'd been talking to David.

'You told Jackie before me?' she said.

'No, it's not like that,' Lata said. 'It just came up.' She took another drink and then tried to change the subject. 'So, David says you're actually going on that trip.'

'Well,' Meena said. 'That's not in stone.'

'Excuse me?' Jackie said.

'Well, it's not definite, is it?'

The aubergine dish was aggressively plain. Jackie took another bite.

'You don't want to go?' David said, oblivious.

'I do,' Meena said. 'It's just, there's work.'

'I don't understand. I thought we'd agreed,' Jackie said.

'It's not that simple.'

It really was.

'Is it the money?' David said. 'Cos–'

'Don't be silly.'

'Honestly, Auntie. It's no problem.'

Meena was going red. She looked down at her plate, her roots showing. Jackie kept eating, if anything, to stop herself from saying something else. It helped that the lamb was so chewy.

There was a silence, or rather, four separate silences. It felt like a scene out of one of Meena's soap operas; the camera showing a close-up of each character before a dramatic cut to the break. Jackie finished her food and excused herself.

With the bathroom door locked behind her, Jackie traced her finger along the top of the cupboard and felt dust. She washed her hands and sat on the toilet even though she didn't need to pee. She opened Twitter, already logged in to her burner account. Then she searched for Sketch.

People were saying horrible things. She clicked a tweet that said 'Not even worth dissing Sketch imo. Everyone knows he's fake as fuck.' Jackie commented: 'You're just jealous of someone with actual talent. Get a life.' She pressed send and then saw her own profile photo next to the comment – a picture of her and Meena from way back, holding the kids – not the anonymous avatar of her burner account. And there was her name. Mother of God. She deleted the comment as fast as she could, but by the time she'd figured out how, it already had a handful of likes.

She felt like she might be sick. Then she got a notification. Someone had tagged her: 'Lmfaaaaoooo @SketchHQ fully got his mum fighting his battles @Jackie_Addo.' They'd screenshotted her comment before she'd deleted it. She wanted to throw her phone out of the window. David would probably be looking at it right now downstairs. Someone would send the screenshot to Chronicle, and he'd use it in another song. David's manager would be furious. She could say she got hacked. She would say she got hacked. Or maybe it would just go away; it could just go away.

She heard music downstairs. She wanted to stay locked in but had a childish thought that if she stayed any longer, they'd think she was doing a poo. She flushed the toilet in case anyone was listening and washed her hands again. She was shaking. Fix up, Jackie! These things happen. Must happen all the time. Something was always happening.

David was probably telling Meena and Lata. They were probably planning an intervention. Maybe travelling alone was a good idea. She could just disappear.

She forced herself down the stairs. Lata and David were in the kitchen, washing up. *Lord see me through.* Was this a panic attack? Had she ruined her son's career? He didn't even look at her. She walked into the living room, expecting Meena to say something horrible. 'It's nice to have a full house again,' she said.

Classic Meena to be all cryptic about it, tease it out. Jackie wanted to be back in the tank, in the dark. She poured herself another drink. Meena nodded at the speakers. 'This is the kind of stuff my parents used to listen to.'

Meena showed her what album was playing: *The Evergreen R. K. Mistry.* The audio was grainy, like old photos. Jackie wished she could go back to the two of them watching those Bollywood films, everything solved with a dance, the kids playing upstairs. She remembered Meena explaining the concept of playback singers, that the actors only mimed singing. It was obvious when you thought about it, like the wrestling matches David used to love, of course it was all fake. But did that change the fun? She thought of the fake meat that David had been eating since going straight edge – sometimes it did.

Meena continued. 'I haven't listened to Mistry in decades. But a few weeks ago – did I tell you this? – the girls at my dance class were talking about her. This new woman had joined, and she said that she knew Mistry well – Mistry was the playback singer the studios went to if they couldn't book Mangeshkar or Bhosle – and this woman said that not only did she know Mistry in the 70s, but that she used to sing for her. Apparently, her voice sounded just like Mistry's and they came up with this scheme. The woman would sing a quarter of Mistry's bookings in secret, at her home studio. This would allow Mistry to take on more bookings and they both made more money. She said the two of them recorded dozens of songs and no one found out. I've been listening to her all week, but I can't hear any difference at all in any of the recordings. This woman must have been lying.'

'Or she was telling the truth and they really did sound the same,' Jackie said.

They sat, drinking their wine and listening to the music, two different realities in the room.

10

David was doing the dishes when his phone buzzed. He dismissed a bunch of notifications and opened the email from his manager with the diss track lyrics attached.

'The devil works fast.'

He forwarded the lyrics to Lata.

'I beg you actually record this,' she said, unable to keep a straight face.

He had a look and could see why she was laughing. The writers were so fucking moist. He watched Lata finish her wine. She set the glass down, a small bit of liquid left at the bottom. His mouth was dry. After thinking it through, he opened the cupboard under the sink, the vodka still in its place. Might even have been the bottle they watered down as teenagers.

He poured two glasses and Lata added lemonade. He paused before taking a sip.

As Lata poured a second – or was this the third? – he put on one of the new instrumentals.

'Time to end this,' he said.

He filmed Lata rapping the diss track lyrics, wearing his cap. She could hardly make it to the end of a line – they were both dying. When she finished, he sent the video to his manager. He was almost tempted to post it on his socials. Would have been fitting, he thought, the creator of his career the one to destroy it. He saw another email from his manager, but before he could read it, his phone died. He could have sworn it had 'Mum' in the subject.

'I'm a triple threat,' Lata said, finishing another glass. 'We're out,' she added, holding up the bottle.

They went into the living room. 'We're going shop,' he told their mums. 'Want anything?'

He avoided his mum's gaze. He didn't want her saying anything about the drinking.

The same guy was behind the till at the corner shop. He went to their school. David remembered playing football with him a couple times. Lata went to get the drinks and for old time's sake, David picked out some sweets. Maybe he could go travelling with his mum in Auntie Meena's place, he thought. It had been years since they'd last gone Ghana. He could reset.

The guy started to babble incoherently, and finally asked for a photo.

'Say less,' David said, going behind the counter, wishing he could remember his name. Lata took the photo and they left, sharing a pack of Magic Stars. He grabbed her arm as they passed the lamppost.

'Close one,' he said.

'Swear down,' she said, sounding like her old self.

'She didn't seem that upset,' David said, as they approached the house. 'Your mum.'

'I don't know. It's like I know she wants me to live this life she couldn't. Don't get me wrong, stuff she had to go through – there weren't exactly options. And here I am, I can do anything, and I choose to quit. Like, I know she sits at home and compares me to you.'

'If it helps,' he said, 'until the music, my mum was always saying I should be more like you.'

He remembered how she'd take out Lata's schoolbooks, and point to different pages, 'Why aren't you doing this?' This one time, he was so annoyed that he took Lata's special pen, the one with the invisible ink, and wrote swear words over a bunch of her books, hoping it would get her in trouble. But nothing ever happened.

Their mums had finished the wine. He'd never really been drunk with his mum, let alone Auntie Meena. She was slouching on the sofa. He hadn't realised how perfect her posture always was until now. Where his mum got quieter, Auntie Meena got more talkative. He poured four glasses. There was old music playing and Lata queued a song.

'You'll like this,' she said.

David sat down and let the three of them talk. He tried to listen but couldn't focus, the edges on everything softening. He looked at Lata. He thought of that meme she used to quote all the time: 'there is much pain in the world but not in this room.'

The song that she put on caught him off guard. It was a slowed & reverb version of the title track from *The Rapture*. His voice was pitched down, and everything was slow-motion, almost unrecognisable. He watched the music video, a short clip from an old anime of a man floating upwards on loop.

'I can finally understand you,' Auntie Meena said, laughing.

Lata hummed along to the song. David's glass was empty, everything moving. He laughed, not sure why. His mum was speaking. His glass was empty again. The music changed and something familiar returned. Came back to him in waves, a song from their childhood. Lata got up to get another drink but when she returned, she didn't sit down. She stood up there, stepped to the left and then the right, and lifted her arms. David rose and moved with her, retreading those old steps, muscle memory kicking in. Instead of watching like they used to, their mums got up to join them. They danced, they dance.

Acknowledgements

——

For reading that first line in 2017 and telling me to keep going, thank you Devi Joshi.

For the edits and guidance, thank you to the teachers and students at Manchester's Centre for New Writing 2016–2019.

For reading my manuscript in July 2020, thank you Maya and Zoe Mahoney, Anne Marie Ryan, Isaac Layton and Haraman Johal.

Thank you to my agent, Laurie Robertson, for taking a chance on this book in October 2020 and for all your help since.

To my teacher and editor, Luke Brown, thank you for encouraging me to send out my first story in 2018, thank you for publishing my first collection in 2022. Your edits transformed this book and I'm forever grateful.

Thank you, Hannah Westland, Graeme Hall, Peter Dyer, Anna-Marie Fitzgerald, Flora Willis, Mila Melia-Kapoor, Angana Narula, Fiona Brown and the team at Serpent's Tail for all your work and support.

For that last minute edit in September 2021, thank you Ravi Mahey.

For a mix of the above and so much more, thank you Sophie Whitehead, Holly Stott and Aashfaria Anwar.

For making this all possible, thank you, Mum, Dad, Nani Ji, Nana Ji, Bibi Ji and Baba Ji.